THE REPRISAL

Laudomia Bonanni

THE REPRISAL

A Novel

Translated by Susan Stewart
and Sara Teardo

THE UNIVERSITY OF CHICAGO PRESS

CHICAGO AND LONDON

LAUDOMIA BONANNI (1907–2002) was one of the preeminent Italian writers of the postwar period, and this is her first book to be translated into English. SUSAN STEWART is the Avalon Foundation University Professor in the Humanities and director of the Society of Fellows in the Liberal Arts at Princeton University. A former MacArthur fellow, she is the author of many books, including poetry collections such as *Red Rover* and *Columbarium*, winner of the National Book Critics Circle Award, and most recently, a work of criticism entitled *The Poet's Freedom*. SARA TEARDO is a lecturer in the Department of French and Italian at Princeton University.

The University of Chicago Press, Chicago 60637
The University of Chicago Press, Ltd., London
© 2013 by The University of Chicago
All rights reserved. Published 2013.
Printed in the United States of America

Originally published as *La rappresaglia* (L'Aquila: Textus, 2003).
© Copyright 2003 Textus s.a.s.

22 21 20 19 18 17 16 15 14 13   1 2 3 4 5

ISBN-13: 978-0-226-06380-5 (cloth)
ISBN-13: 978-0-226-01830-0 (e-book)

The University of Chicago Press gratefully acknowledges the generous financial support of the Italian Ministry of Foreign Affairs, through the Italian Cultural Institute of Chicago, toward the publication of this book. La University of Chicago Press ringrazia il Ministero degli Affari Esteri italiano per il generoso sostegno finanziario fornito, tramite l'Istituto Italiano di Cultura di Chicago, alla pubblicazione di questo libro.

Library of Congress Cataloging-in-Publication Data

Bonanni, Laudomia, 1907–2002.
    [Rappresaglia. English]
    The reprisal : a novel / Laudomia Bonanni ; translated by Susan Stewart and Sara Teardo.
        pages ; cm
    ISBN 978-0-226-06380-5 (hardcover : alkaline paper) — ISBN 978-0-226-01830-0 (e-book) I. Title.
    PQ4807.O555R3713 2013
    853'.914 — dc23

                                        2012027710

♾ This paper meets the requirements of ANSI/NISO Z39.48–1992 (Permanence of Paper).

a Pietro Zullino

(1936–2012)

CONTENTS

INTRODUCTION

La rappresaglia is the final work of the novelist Laudomia Bonanni, who was considered in the period after World War II to be one of the most promising Italian writers of realist fiction. Bonanni was born in 1907 in L'Aquila, a medieval city approximately sixty miles due east of Rome in the Abruzzo region of Central Italy; she died in Rome in 2002. Bonanni held that a writer is a "fearless spectator," and in all of her work she pursued certain timeless themes: the loss of childhood innocence; the Italian veneration of, and ambivalence toward, the power of maternity; the intricacy of human bonds in even the smallest of communities; the struggle against contingency in the poor mountain region that was her birthplace. Today her stories and novels are of interest not only to students of Italian literature but also to a new generation of specialists in women's studies and scholars of European twentieth-century fiction. With this translation, completed with the collaboration of Bonanni's descendents and scholars in L'Aquila, we present *La rappresaglia* to English-language readers for the first time.

From a family of modest background, her father a musician and coal merchant and her mother an elementary school teacher, Bonanni was named for a character in *Niccoló de' Lapi*, a historical novel by Massimo D'Azeglio.[1] She, too, trained as a teacher of young children and from the age of seventeen worked in the remote mountain village schools of the Abruzzo before returning, in 1930, to her native province of L'Aquila. During her teenage years she published her first collection of fiction, *Storie tragiche della montagna. Novelle d'Abruzzo* (Tragic stories from the mountains: Novellas of the Abruzzo; 1927) and she tried her hand at children's literature in the period of her teaching career.

Bonanni had an equally long career as a writer for magazines and newspapers. In 1927 as well, she published her first article, an essay for an education journal. From then until 1983, when she discontinued her journalism, she wrote more than 1,300 pieces, often revising and reframing earlier work. Yet more than twenty years passed before she came to national prominence as a writer of fiction. She won a national literary contest in 1948, the Amici della domenica prize, for her long stories "Il fosso" (The ditch) and "Il mostro" ("The Monster"); they were collected in 1949 in a single printed volume, *Il fosso*, and augmented by two more stories, "Messa funebre" (Funeral mass) and "Il seme" (The seed).

Three of the fictions of *Il fosso* were based in the often harsh circumstances of the village life she observed before and during the war—the exception is "Il mostro," which is a story of an adolescent in a middle-class family. Designed for an adult literary audience, the stories led to her first real success: the manuscript was published by the prestigious press Mondadori, and she was praised by many important critics and writers, including the poet and Nobel laureate Eugenio Montale, who compared her realism, with its precise attention to local detail, to James Joyce's. The volume went on to receive the Premio Bagutta Opera Prima in 1950—the first instance of this first-book prize going to a woman.

1. Sandra Petrignani, *Le signore della scrittura. Interviste* (Milan: La Tartaruga, 1984), 59–64.

In quick succession, Bonanni was able to publish more volumes: the collection *Palma e sorelle* (Palma and sisters), which appeared in 1954 and won the Premio Soroptimist, and the novels *L'imputata* (The accused; 1960) and *L'adultera* (The adulteress; 1964). These, too, were published by a major press—Bompiani, founded by a former editor at Mondadori—and received several national awards; *L'imputata* won the Premio Viareggio, considered by many to be the most important literary prize in Italy, and *L'adultera* won the Premio Selezione Campiello. In almost every case, her novels were written in tandem with her journalistic writing and often their plots were derived from newspaper and magazine pieces she had researched and written.

Exhausted from all of her activities and suffering from a recurring acute depression, Bonanni retired from teaching in 1966. Leaving L'Aquila, she moved to Rome, where she sought out literary circles, especially the salon of the prominent critic Maria Bellonci and her husband Goffredo, a group she had first met in 1948 when this "Salotto Bellonci" awarded her their Amici della domenica prize. In their company she discovered a social life rooted in literature. She later recounted in an interview, "I found myself among the myths of Italian literature of the 40s and 50s: [Gianna] Manzini, la [Anna] Banti, [Alberto] Moravia, [Emilio] Cecchi, la [Elsa] Morante."[2] She wrote a number of articles about the beauty of the Roman landscape and the Roman spring. But by the end of the 1960s, she felt she had lost the attention of critics and that the arc of her success had begun to decline. She again experienced a period of isolation and serious depression.

Then, in the '70s, she began to publish again, often consolidating articles and shorter pieces into longer volumes. She brought out four more works: nonfiction essays stemming from her twenty years of service, during and after the war, as a lay judge with the Abruzzo Juvenile Court, gathered in the volume *Vietato ai minori* (Forbid-

2. Ibid., 61.

den to minors; 1974); a collection of short stories set during the war years and immediately after, *Città del tabacco* (Tobacco city; 1977); and two more novels, *Il bambino di pietra* (The stone baby; 1979) and *Le droghe* (The drugs; 1982). She was nominated for the Premio Strega, another highly regarded Italian literary prize, in 1960, 1975, and again in 1979.

Nevertheless, these steady successes after her relatively late start as a writer met with an abrupt disappointment in 1985 when Bompiani unexpectedly returned the manuscript of *La rappresaglia,* asking Bonanni for revisions that she was unwilling to make. She refused to allow Bompiani to republish her earlier writing or publish her later work, rejecting the premises of a commercial press.[3] She went into seclusion again, where she remained until her death.[4]

Our translation of *La rappresaglia* is based on the 2003 Textus edition, published posthumously in L'Aquila and edited by Carlo De Matteis. A letter Bonanni wrote in 1985 to Bellonci, asking her to intervene with Bompiani on the book's behalf, gives evidence of her commitment to the text as she left it at that time. Yet there is emerging evidence that Bonanni may have worked on the novel for almost forty years.[5] In the immediate postwar period she published various articles and short narratives about the war and it seems to have remained a source of inspiration for her work until the end of her life.[6]

3. Pietro Zullino, *La vita e l'opera di Laudomia Bonanni* (Rome: privately printed, 2002), 159.

4. The fullest account of Bonanni's biography can be found in Gianfranco Giustizieri, *Io che ero una donna di domani* (L'Aquila: Edizioni del Consiglio Regionale dell'Abruzzo, 2008), 9–29.

5. Laudomia Bonanni, *Epistolario*, vol. 1, ed. Fausta Samaritani (Lanciano: Carabba, 2006), 124.

6. Bonanni's family house and existing papers were severely damaged in the 2009 earthquake that nearly destroyed the city of L'Aquila, and our knowledge of the circumstances of the writing of the novel has been limited by this tragic situation.

Indeed, with her teacher/narrator, who has an intimate knowledge of village life during the war and yet remains alienated and somewhat remote, Bonanni has drawn a self-portrait of her situation as an observer, transcriber, and judge of the moral life around her.

In 1949 the national magazine *Noi donne* (We women) published an interview with Bonanni that mentioned she was working on a forthcoming narrative fiction called *Stridor di denti* (Gnashing of teeth). No copy of this novel, in manuscript or print form, has ever been found, but from a letter to Mondadori from this period we know that the manuscript was finished in 1949 and that her initial submission to the press was rejected because "the work did not demonstrate the expressive completeness of *Il fosso*."[7] In a 1949 letter to Bellonci, Bonanni mentions a back-up plan to submit the manuscript to an international literary contest sponsored by the New York publisher Harper Brothers; she expresses her fear that the unspecified topic "might seem communist" and might not appeal to an American audience.[8]

"Gnashing of teeth" is the well-known phrase from Matthew 13:42, where unrepentant sinners are described as "weeping and gnashing [their] teeth" as they are condemned during the final harrowing of the righteous. The phrase is mentioned by the protagonist of *La rappresaglia* and a number of Bonanni scholars have come to concur with Fausta Samaritani's suggestion that Bonanni may have returned, during the 1980s, to this manuscript from the postwar years and used it as the foundation for her novel.[9] We can find further proof of the duration of her commitment to the novel in a piece she published in *Il Giornale d'Italia* in 1952, "Una donna fra le mogli" (Woman between the wives), that anticipates an identical

7. Laudomia Bonanni, *Epistolario*, vol. 2, CD-ROM, compiled by Fausta Samaritani, 2011.
8. Bonanni, *Epistolario*, 1:90.
9. Ibid., 30, 87, 90, 232; Giustizieri, *Io che ero una donna di domani*, 58–69.

episode in *La rappresaglia* and outlines the plot of the story.[10] In a 1955 article, "Gli innocenti" (The innocents), in the same journal, she also uses the expression "stridor di denti." Here she refers to the tragic consequences of the war, noting how it has weighed upon younger generations and contending that "every ferocity committed by men, consciously or not, affects a child."[11] *La rappresaglia* therefore may be the work of art that most fully indicates the entirety of Bonanni's thought and formal artistry across the course of her career.

The central action of *La rappresaglia* takes place during the particularly harsh winter months of December 1943 and January 1944. The story is then extended through a frame tale that reaches well into the postwar period. With armistice declared on September 8, 1943, the Italians were presented with a confusing mandate: they were to cease any acts of hostility toward the Anglo-American forces and react "with maximum decision" against any offensives coming "from any other quarter whatsoever." There was no specific mention of the Germans, but the Germans immediately strengthened their occupation. By October 13, the Italian government declared outright war on Germany, and the German general Albert Kesselring was assigned to organize Nazi forces along the "Gustav Line," a defense that ran from the Garigliano River in Campania through Cassino to the Sangro River on the Adriatic coast. With this formation, the Germans cut the Abruzzo region in two, making maximum use of the region's natural geography of mountains, hills, and ravines.[12] The Allies broke through to Cassino nine months later in May 1944. Between the late autumn of 1943 and the spring of 1944, the region was controlled by the Germans and Mussolini's

10. Giustizieri, *Io che ero una donna di domani*, 63 passim.
11. Recorded in ibid., 148.
12. Walter Cavalieri, *L'Aquila: dall'armistizio alla Repubblica: 1943–1946* (L'Aquila: Edizioni Studio 7, 1994).

puppet government, headquartered at the town of Salò on Lake Garda.

The Germans and their Fascist collaborators kept up a constant barrage of combings, attacks, and retaliations against the local populations, and many villages along the line were evacuated and razed to the ground. Many villagers, disaffected soldiers of the Italian army, and refugees from Rome and other urban areas, including persecuted Jews, went into hiding in the area's remote farmhouses, outbuildings, caves, and forests. Prisoners once held in concentration camps, including the mostly Australian and New Zealand troops imprisoned in nearby Acquafredda and assigned to road and mine work, had been able to flee after the armistice, frequently with the complicity of their Italian guards. Some of these refugees became active in the resistance and paid with their lives. Reprisals were rampant. As early as late September, a group of young Aquilani seized some weapons and left the city to join the partisans but were denounced to the Germans by the local fascists. Nine of these rebels, armed, were captured and secretly executed. Their death is now commemorated in the Piazza IX Martiri in L'Aquila.[13]

This, then, is the milieu of Bonanni's novel. As was her usual practice, she took inspiration from the local news, in print and oral tradition, and from her own experiences during the war. Bonanni signed, as all teachers were required to do, the Fascist Party card; she was the provincial representative for the women's section of the Fascist Party and her appointment to the juvenile court came about under the Fascist government. Like many Socialists, including her father, she had felt an initial enthusiasm for the party, but by the end of the war she was completely disillusioned with both Fascist ideology and practice. Her sympathy with the Left and the feminist ideals of her partisan protagonist La Rossa is evident. Nevertheless, no his-

---

13. See Corrado Colacito, *I martiri aquilani del 23 settembre 1943* (L'Aquila: Textus, 1996).

torical evidence exists for the story she narrates here of a pregnant prisoner's ordeal at the hands of a band of fascist misfits who wait to execute her until she gives birth to her child. Some of the particular circumstances of the novel resemble developments recorded in the diary of Bonanni's brother-in-law Corrado Colacito, which was first published in 1944 under the title *Sotto il tallone tedesco* (Under the German heel) as a chronicle of the ten-month-long occupation of the village of Caramanico Terme by the Germans.[14] Yet the novel remains a work of her imagination.

Rather than simply juxtapose fascist thuggery to La Rossa's social idealism, Bonanni creates a narrative of considerable moral complexity. Its tragic theme of revenge, sacrifice, and justice emerges as a universal one, reaching back to the conclusion of the *Oresteia*. The work moves with all the swiftness of classical tragedy and, like those in such tragedies, her characters suffer from a lack of self-knowledge. Two of the fascist band — the leader Vanzi, called Il Nero, and the former security guard Franzè — seem, even in these isolated circumstances, to be drawn to structures of power and relish participating in their cause. But the remaining men of the group — the old farmer Baboro, whose son Baborino has been murdered by anti-fascists under unknown circumstances; the pig gelder Alleluia, with his taste for violence; the shoemaker Divinangelo; the farmer/laborer/cook and family man Annaloro; and the nameless schoolteacher narrator — have all passively accepted the Fascist Party card, supposedly for practical reasons.

As the novel begins, they are hiding out in the mountains while the war comes to a close — to "see how the dust will settle." They come upon La Rossa by accident and although they quickly condemn her to death through a "war tribunal" that is in truth a kangaroo court, they are divided in their judgments and she almost survives a sec-

14. Corrado Colacito, *Sotto il tallone tedesco: Cronaca di un paese d'Abruzzo* (L'Aquila: Textus, 2005).

ond trial before the vote is tipped against her. The balance between accident and judgment is the very hinge of the novel—not only as a plotted account of events but also as a work of moral and theological speculation. The Italian word, *rappresaglia*, from the Latin *reprehendere*, to take again, to retake, indicates the complex chain of circumstances that led the men's passive fear of retaliation to be turned into an active exercise of retaliation. We never learn what acts they have committed in the past that may have led them to fear reprisals, and we are never certain that the acts they are revenging have any relation to their victim. Yet this is the bitter logic of the reprisal: any eye serves as recompense for an eye and any tooth serves as recompense for a tooth. A highly localized economy is at work with its own, absurd sense of "justice."

The fatal tipping vote is cast by the novel's remarkable child character, Nirli, a boy on the cusp of adolescence who follows his neighbor Divinangelo into membership in the band after he is orphaned and ineradicably burned by a fire in which his father, an elderly bibliophile, is killed. The men and Nirli himself believe that the fire was set by the partisans because Germans had confiscated space in the house. But Bonanni does not present a straightforward account of causes, and we are led to consider that La Rossa has been unjustly accused of this crime. A second justification for the execution of a partisan is the murder of Baboro's son Baborino. We learn that La Rossa in fact has killed, in the course of an earlier accidental encounter, a villager whom she refers to generically as "a Baborino" or "the other Baborino." Whether he is the same man remains ambiguous.

An intense, yet ambivalent, relationship grows—one of hatred and near-maternal/filial love—between Nirli and La Rossa and reaches its culmination in the novel's dramatic last passages. These two characters, both by birth outsiders to the ragtag band of fascists, are linked by the narrative to a third stranger: Don Antonio—a young peasant turned seminarian who wanders, perhaps by chance or perhaps after hearing rumors of the woman prisoner, into the mountain monastery where the fascists are hiding. The priest decides to stay on in case he is needed to administer last rites to La Rossa. If, from the viewpoint of theology, the doctrines of forgiveness and resurrection with their promises of reversal suggest there can be no Christian tragedy, we find the resolutely secular La Rossa resisting every entreaty from the priest. Motivated to save her soul at death, he fails miserably, from his point of view, to do so and at the same time he is deeply affected and influenced by her.

Admittedly a "red," La Rossa proclaims the powers of "the people who use a hammer and chisel on the great collective head, to open it once and for all." Indeed, she is more given to theological and spiritual speculation than is the priest, who adheres to doctrine. She proclaims her "love for all mankind," and she has thought a great deal about the role of women in revolution. She observes that "revolution too is obscene and bloody because of love. It is consumed by love. Revolution is a woman, it gives birth by itself the way I do. . . . I am the revolution." In an argument close to Hannah Arendt's claims for the spontaneity and natality of genuine political processes, La Rossa's position is that revolution is both imminent and utopian.[15] Yet earlier circumstances have made her into a killer; now, alone with her pregnancy, her two first children long dead, she is shut off from the "Sallesi," the women of the partisan family who sheltered her, and she cannot resist aggravating the men who have imprisoned her. She finds herself railing against the young priest and tormenting the boy even as the three of them gradually develop relationships of considerable emotional and spiritual depth — an exchange that counters both unthought dogma and blind obedience to authority.

Shadowing the work as a whole is the fundamental difference between the teacher/narrator's passive, often uncomprehending, tran-

15. Hannah Arendt, *Between Past and Future: Eight Exercises in Political Thought* (New York: Viking, 1961), 166; and *The Life of the Mind* (New York: Harcourt, 1971), 127.

scription of his diurnal, more properly nocturnal, notes from the period and the homegrown writings of La Rossa, those treasured thoughts she has recorded in a small notebook she carries with her at all times. Refusing to carry a gun, the teacher has been assigned the job of watchman over the prisoner and hence is a witness to much of her speech, which he faithfully records. He has the first and last words of the novel and whatever we know of other characters is filtered through his viewpoint. La Rossa's notebook, in contrast, despite her pleas to the seminarian to promise to preserve it, vanishes — the pages are rapidly and heedlessly burned in order to provide a warm fire for her infant.

Bonanni creates a quiet contrast between the teacher's claims regarding the narrative and the novel's actual form. He muses, "Why keep all these papers? . . . Sheet after sheet: pages of a diary, scattered observations, long transcripts like the kind made from tape-recordings, notes on torn bits of paper . . . . Why keep it all inside for forty years? A historian, so to speak, a biographer or a simple chronicler. I'll try only to put the whole thing back together." The novel, however, despite its careful historical and regional detail, manifests the formal integrity of a prose poem. Bonanni organizes the work's hundred and forty tightly focused pages into ten chapters, each composed of six numbered sections of equal length. With this method she gives her Inferno something of the rhythm of a collection of cantos.

The novel's first-person narration is unusual in her oeuvre[16] and her style throughout is sober and economical. It is also filled with colloquial language. La Rossa's speech especially mixes the fixed phrases of an autodidact with wildly inventive curses, hectoring diatribes, and quiet reflections. The boy struggles between the learned milieu of his early childhood and his desire to sound like the men

16. She also uses the first person in her late novels *Il bambino di pietra* (The stone baby; 1979) and *Le droghe* (The drugs; 1982).

with whom his fate has been cast: his wolf cry and a number of other paralinguistic sounds and gestures demonstrate how close the group of misfits has come to the bedrock of an existence in the elements.

The novel is suffused with subtle and interwoven images. The nocturnal trial scene evokes the lighting of Caravaggio, as does a later scene of the teacher writing by candlelight; the child's scars and thin clothing are juxtaposed to the flaming hair and thick skirts of the partisan woman, and his innocent enthusiasm for violence finds its counterpart above all in her sarcastic, measured language. The extremity of the outpost brings forward the intersections between human and animal existence; hunger, thirst, and illness are enemies of the characters as much as any rival factions. Bonanni constantly emphasizes the band's painful contact with a hostile earth and air; shoes and boots and La Rossa's winter cloak acquire a looming significance as intermediaries and means of survival.

Yet we are reminded that the eternal return of the "chain" of vengeance and murder for its own sake is a human invention. Christianity's veneration of the mother of the sacrificed child is reframed in wartime as violence against the sacrificial mother. The men are afraid of the partisan's feminine, Fury-like, power, afraid of birth, and the maieutic capacity of tragedy to bring forward what was hidden is brilliantly explored. At the same time, they are transformed by their meager preparations for a Christmas feast; the rituals of that birth celebration in the midst of the winter dark, sustained by a visit from shepherd bagpipers playing carols, show them at their most human.

Perhaps most vividly, Bonanni brings forward the physical environment of the abandoned mountain monastery, refuge of an occasional hermit, where the events unfold. Within the vertical orientation of the mountains, she describes this building as tucked into the rock wall itself; its abandoned choirs and altars have a purgatorial aspect, poised between the earthly paradise of the home and village and the hellish uncertainty of the caves and sheepfolds higher up the range, where there is no way of knowing whether an encounter will be with hostile or friendly forces. The monastery seems to be based upon Eremo Santo Spirito, an actual sanctuary in the Maiella Mountains, in the rocky township of Roccamorice, approximately forty miles from L'Aquila. Bonanni gives a cavernous dimension to the internal spaces of this monastery that was built from an original hermit-monk's cave as she also conveys the precipitous feeling of its perch on the mountain. It was a place she knew well, often taking walks there, and its physical plan closely matches the structure she describes.[17]

Fire and snow, constantly evoked, also become something like characters in the novel. The men gather each day around the fire in the kitchen, and they must keep the fire going as well in the often-locked room of the woman prisoner, twigs and branches must be gathered continually to feed the flames, and the ash of each night's fire must be kept hot so that the morning fire will glow and rekindle. This cycle of interior intensification and diminishment affects and models the rising and falling cycles of moods and speech taking place near the fires. And La Rossa, with her "flaming gaze" and red hair, embodies its powerful heat.

In contrast, the snow is described as descending from a glassy sky — as if a divinity were looking down through that transparency, an image of conscience even as the snow relentlessly grows and hardens in parallel to the increasing resolve and hardened hearts of the men who will become a firing squad. Collectively and individually, the men become trapped by the snow and their terrible decision. Early in the novel, Bonanni describes "the first snow: late, difficult, and bitter" under a sky like "glass." Later the men fear the full advent of "the great snow, plentiful and peaceful, which protects the seeds beneath the earth and the first green shoots of grain" with its accompaniment of "sleet and stiff winds from the north." As the birth of the child begins, the snow becomes "high, but still soft, you

17. Giustizieri, *Io che ero una donna di domani*, 68.

could sink up to your knees." And when La Rossa is condemned irrevocably, the men awaken to a swarming light beyond the monastery windows and "a full heavy wave of snow from the coast . . . piling up in dunes." Nirli, who has pronounced the final death sentence, "plunged in with his boots. His wolf cub's cry died without an echo." Like the betraying figures of Dante's ninth circle of Hell, the men are paralyzed in their motion by the ever-hardening crust of ice encasing themselves and their world. The night before the execution, La Rossa explains to the priest that "the cold could take off your very skin. A starry sky that crunches. The sky is a pane of glass, the stars are screeching against it, and it will break into pieces. The sky itself is weeping and gnashing its teeth." The final killing ground is described with its footprints scattered in every direction and the snow "dirty with trodden blood" while, inside, the fire out irrevocably, "only a little black ash remained."

Writing of a pair of 1920–1921 killings of pregnant young women civilians, the first with a child in her arms, by British and, later, IRA soldiers in the aftermath of the Irish rebellion of 1916, Michael Wood suggests that this multiple atrocity—the killing of a civilian, of a woman, of a mother, of a child in the womb—happens "in a world without rules but where it still feels as if rules are being broken." He goes on to say, "The word 'revenge' is a symptom of this in-between state, and there was a more current contemporary word: reprisal." He writes of how reprisals, those random killings of civilians after a member of an army is killed, combine "causality and chance. There is a reason why this is happening, but no reason why it is happening to you." He draws a conclusion of much relevance to Bonanni's novel: "reprisals offer . . . a narrative that doesn't know its own limits or procedures and so isn't entirely a narrative: a logic that seems broken even before it starts to operate."[18] Bonanni's careful,

18. Michael Wood, *Yeats and Violence* (Oxford: Oxford University Press, 2010), 22–24.

ten-part, measured structure for her work, enfolding a plot full of accidents, loose ends, coincidences, and multiple causalities, perfectly expresses this self-justifying unjustified logic. We are left wondering if the young German soldier Hans set Nirli's family house ablaze with a carelessly dropped cigarette, if La Rossa killed Baboro's Baborino or someone else, if her own death was brought about by a hemorrhage or the firing squad, and if the bitter, often bizarre deaths of the surviving fascists — all of them unable to father children in the postwar years — were brought about by the reprisals of fate or the gods. Tragedy transmutes accident into form and in *La rappresaglia* Bonanni has done no less.

A NOTE ON THE TRANSLATION

Throughout *La rappresaglia*, Laudomia Bonanni uses what the editor Carlo De Matteis has called an "ascetic" style that drains the syntax. At the same time, her language is enlivened by colloquialisms and textured by archaisms. We have followed her style as closely as possible, which means that we have maintained her complex use of tense; she often mixes tenses in a single paragraph, and we occasionally have used the past progressive tense for the simple past in order to show that the narrator is picturing the scene—this is an obvious feature of his narration and he often slips all the way into the present tense, showing the continuity of the past with his present thoughts. The effects of a temporal palimpsest become a crucial aspect of his perspective. Bonanni also often proceeds without clarifying the referents of her pronouns and terms. At other times, she introduces a scene over several paragraphs, describing attributes and effects of an action without naming the agent. Because Italian and English possessive pronouns work differently, our bias was to be more specific than the original. We have looked for equivalent English terms for the novel's curses, proverbs, songs, and vernacular expressions. Nevertheless, a few passages may need clarification.

As the scene of the action is modeled on the monastery of Acquafredda in Santo Spirito a Maiella, the native town of the fascist band resembles Caramanico Terme, a mountain village in the province of Pescara, crossed by the Orfento Valley and bordering the spurs of the Maiella and Morrone mountains.[1] La Rapina, mentioned first on page 42, refers to the mountain pass of Fonte Tettone that in World War II was controlled, for its strategic position, by the Germans. A cableway formerly used for the transport of wood and coal and later deployed by the Germans to transport supplies and ammunition was located there.[2] The fugitives mentioned on page 44 and throughout the novel would have included the Jews fleeing to escape deportation, as described on pages 46 and 128. When, during the armistice, the Acquafredda prisoners of war who had been forced to work in mines and road construction looked for refuge, they turned to the local villages, the shepherds' caves in the Maiella and Morrone mountains, the empty caves of hermits, and abandoned monasteries such as the one in the novel. Many tried to cross the lines to reach the armies of the Allies.[3]

On page 63, the narrator describes La Rossa quoting Herodotus, but the expression "War is the mother of all things" is a transposition of Heracleitus's fragment 53— "War is both father and king of all; some he has shown forth as gods and others as men, some he has made slaves and others free"—and thus a poignant substitution of "mother" for "father." The passage thereby also illustrates the teacher's fallibility. He loosely alludes, on page 70, to a passage from Revelations 3:16— "So then because thou art lukewarm, and neither cold nor hot, I will spew thee out of my mouth"—as he reflects upon his somewhat alienated membership in the band.

1. Giustizieri, *Io che ero una donna di domani*, 65.
2. Ibid.
3. Ibid., 66.

La Rossa's confused mention of the Vandeans on page 72 refers to the brutally suppressed 1793–1796 royalist uprising of Roman Catholics of the Vendée against the secular Republican government of the French Revolution. She points to this combat as a historical instance of genocide as she predicts a coming genocide after the war. It is not clear that she understands that this incident involved the murder of Roman Catholics by revolutionaries—an example that would hardly seem apropos. Perhaps Bonanni is suggesting, as she has elsewhere, that La Rossa's autodidacticism has led her to misunderstand history. The "pronunciation of D'Annunzio" on page 80 refers to the antiquated terms "Inghilesi" and "Todeschi," used instead of the modern "Inglesi" and "Tedeschi" by the turn-of-the-twentieth-century Abruzzese poet, journalist, and novelist Gabriele D'Annunzio.[4]

The image of villages in flames and people in a lineup described on page 124 recalls the Filetto slaughter, in the Abruzzese mountains—an episode Bonanni described in a 1969 article, "Le donne di Filetto" (The women of Filetto). It refers to the June 1944 German reprisal in retaliation for a partisan attack. Despite the protests of one of their officers, who was consequently accused of collaboration and shot, the Germans rounded up and killed seventeen men. The corpses were dragged into a stable and burned before the rest of the village was sacked and set afire.[5]

On page 140, the Dante quote is taken from the *Divine Comedy*: "L'aiuola che ci fa tanto feroci,/volgendom' io con li etterni Gemelli,/tutta m'apparve da' colli a le foci;/poscia rivolsi li occhi a li occhi belli." (*Paradiso* 22.151–54. In the prose translation of Charles Singleton: "The little threshing-floor which makes us so/fierce

4. Specifically, in his prose works *Il compagno dagli occhi senza cigli* and *Il libro segreto*.
5. Gianfranco Giustizieri, *Laudomia scrittrice senza tempo* (Lanciano: Carabba, 2010), 79–88.

was all revealed to me from hills to river-/mouths, as I circled with the eternal Twins./Then to the beauteous eyes I turned my eyes/ again.")[6]

Susan Stewart
Sara Teardo
Princeton, New Jersey

6. Dante Alighieri, *The Divine Comedy*, trans. Charles S. Singleton. *Paradiso*, vol. 1 (Princeton, NJ: Princeton University Press, 1975), 255.

ACKNOWLEDGMENTS

This translation is dedicated, with deepest affection, to the memory of the journalist, novelist, and historian Pietro Zullino, who, to our great surprise, first introduced us and later encouraged us to undertake our work. Pietro's sustaining friendship, sense of humor, and lifelong commitment to Bonanni's writing have been an inspiration.

We were aided by many other scholars and citizens of L'Aquila as well. Bonanni's heir and literary executor Gianfranco Colacito has assisted us in many ways, and we are grateful for the invaluable help of the biographer and critic Gianfranco Giustizieri and the hospitality of his kind family. We also thank Giuliano Tomassi and Elpidio Valeri for their insights regarding Bonanni's legacy. In Rome, we were inspired by conversations with Fausta Samaritani and Gabriela Marsili Marazzita. Rita Bertoni provided precious information about the milieu of the novel and has been one of our most engaged readers.

Princeton University has been forthcoming with research assistance for each of us and we have benefited from the interest and literary friendship of our colleagues in the departments of French and Italian and English.

We have appreciated the continuing support of our editor at the University of Chicago Press, Alan Thomas. Oonagh Stransky kindly read the final draft of our translation with great care and enthusiasm and made a number of valuable suggestions. The photographer Giovanni Lattanzi has generously allowed us to reproduce his photograph of the Eremo di Santo Spirito a Maiella — the mountain refuge where the novel is set. It can also be found online at http://foto .inabruzzo.it.

THE REPRISAL

I

1. These facts have never been revealed. No one has ever breathed a word. Everything buried. Soon the last shovelful of dirt will drop, so to speak, since I, the last, am old. It's incredible how once you're in your seventies, you tumble toward your eighties. And for years I have been asking myself if I'm obliged to exhume those facts. If it would make any sense. Or come to any good. It is just a story like any other war story, and would be a lousy one at that if women and children hadn't been involved. Women make for tragedy. And children are the lamb.

That cursed day we set out for the hermitage of Acquafredda. Armed, of course, and with knapsacks and blanket rolls and a mule loaded down with supplies. But at that point it was no expedition and it was not yet an escape. It still could have turned into a temporary exile, to allow the dust to settle or come to an end. Even wars come to an end. (I believed that, then.)

Pilgrims would go up there, shepherds would pass by on their way elsewhere, and a few hunters would show up; in the summer it was a favorite spot for picnickers carrying baskets and jugs of wine. In peacetime. And that July there had been a camp organized for fascist youth, and people said they were firing guns to train boys for war. It hadn't been used as a monastery for fifty years, but anyone

3

could take shelter and cook and spend the night. It was a sort of mountain refuge. From time to time the hermit — an old man, a lunatic — showed up, and then vanished. But at that time, nobody was there. And we could still go back.

The woman was what blocked us.

2. I began. And I must have always known I would. Otherwise, why keep all these papers. Why bring them with me when I was fleeing through the mountains, the only weight in my knapsack, as if they were all I needed to survive. A pile of papers. Sheet after sheet: pages of a diary, scattered observations, long transcripts like the kind made from tape recordings, notes on torn bits of paper. Registered by fingers numb from the cold, often at night by candlelight. And at my back, I felt the impatient presence of someone else in the cell, another's breath and that incessant rustling of the straw mattress. And, until it broke, the screeching and grumbling of the radio.

Why keep it all inside for forty years? A historian, so to speak, a biographer or a simple chronicler. I'll try only to put the whole thing back together. And as I go ahead, I'll be shedding a burden. A confession, maybe? In any case, a testimony. And for whom? Maybe only for me.

No, this is not compensation for the frustrations of a writer who missed his calling. More exactly, a failed writer. By that time, when I set out on that risky misadventure, I'd given up any ambition. All my efforts had come to a few short stories published in a couple of provincial journals, a little poetry book printed at my own expense, some novels in a drawer. All already set aside. To go in the trash. These notebooks that I am about to fill will be found after my death. By the woman who will have been taking care of me — one of the many women who hire themselves out keeping house for bachelors — or by the priest called at the last minute (to whom I will not have confessed), or by whoever will take care of emptying the house. Clearing out rags and papers. Papers that belonged to an old schoolteacher and therefore are useless. Good to light a fire. They will never be read.

3. The very day we arrived at Acquafredda—after traveling in the dark for five hours, with the child swaying sleepily between the sacks loaded on the mule's back—exactly on that same day, the woman was caught. All of us were still wandering the monastery—except Franzè, out on reconnaissance—orienting ourselves, opening the small rickety doors of the cells, inspecting the straw mattresses, setting out our bags and provisions: when we heard the blast of a rifle. It echoed like a shootout.

And shortly after, Franzè appeared in the churchyard, pushing her forward from behind with the rifle he'd been issued as a guardsman. The prisoner was in front, hefty, wrapped up to her eyes in a peasant's cloak, with him following, bouncing on his feet, the barrel of his weapon pointed at her back. Behind him was the child, who had been the first to run outside. He was hopping on his skinny, miserable, blood-red legs, like the legs of a skinned goat, and was pulling a donkey loaded with loose bundles of kindling along by the halter.

Raising strange cries that ricocheted awhile in a gloomy echo, the men went out and crowded around. They had recognized the woman. I recognized her, too. A stranger recently arrived in the village, supposedly escaping the bombing in the city. She was staying with the Sallesi, but not in hiding. On the contrary, she seemed to be helping the family in the fields with the last chores of the season. Even so, she was not a peasant. And there she was, dressed just like a peasant, wrapped in the black cloak up to the white flash of her darting eyes.

Surprise and, soon, alarm silenced the cries. They were strange, excited. Like when a prostitute arrives before the troop.

"Uh, and now we start with the women," grumbled Annaloro, who had far too many in his household.

5

And Alleluia, the farm boy, yelled, "the slut!"—his blushing neck swelling.

They were all addressing Vanzi's bald head, which had appeared behind the window bars. Nobody spoke to me; they were already avoiding my gaze. I was among them, and yet, it was as if they couldn't see me.

The child shouted first. "These bundles of sticks are full of rifles and cartridges!"

That meant weapons for everybody. And they started shouting again.

Vanzi gave the order to take her inside. They followed, dumbstruck. The woman went straight to the kitchen, as if she knew the place (and in fact she did), and sat on one of the benches at either side of the fireplace where fresh-cut logs burned, sizzling and hissing. She spread her legs open under her wide pleated skirt and lifted it up, stretching out her two big feet in their cowhide shoes toward the fire.

"Nice shoes, eh? What shoes the partisans have!" burst out Franzè. His were all worn out.

The woman bared her head. A head covered in cropped hair that reared up like snakes. She was not young: two white streaks on her temples and harsh lines around her mouth. Everyone was staring at her, following her hands as she pulled back the cloak. As if a monument had been uncovered. She was a monument indeed.

When she took off the cloak and threw it on the ground, her belly became visible.

And it seemed enormous.

4. From that moment, cursing broke out, like a reaction to the unexpected and sinister events.

"Goddamn it!" shouted little Divinangelo, looking at the others. "She is pregnant, this slut."

The woman spat on the fire and promptly retorted, "So? Your sperm couldn't get a cat pregnant."

Only the child laughed, an outsized laugh, writhing wildly. His stretched vocal chords were like a blood clot beneath the stain, bright red, also there on his neck. The men tried not to look at his scars. He was sitting on the bench across from the woman. Spreading his toes, he was exposing his pale little feet to the fire; he had taken off his pigskin shoes and his thick, mended socks. "Goddamn it," he repeated in a shrill imitation, ready to dodge any punishing slap. He was running his hands over his glossy, skinned, legs, already bitten by the cold. Someone later remembered that she had been looking at the child's legs without uttering a word: any other woman would have asked.

The little kid said haughtily, "When we execute you, I'll take your shoes." Before this, nobody had thought of the idea of an execution.

Then, old Baboro stood up from the corner where he had retreated. He was like a patriarch, with his long beard and the black cloak he never took off: signs of his mourning.

The woman glanced at him and at the same time answered the kid: "You'll stick my shoes up your butt."

"Goddamn it," he repeated with a child's annoying insistence, his ears as red as a rooster's comb. He said it with half his mouth, a word that had been chewed unwillingly and too long. (The uncomfortable feeling a child has whenever he tries on a grown-up's clothing.) Nobody thought of correcting him and, yellow around the nostrils, he displayed his arrogant look in vain. He had already gone feral.

5. Nobody had yet thought about the night in there. Or maybe we were all thinking about it, the child included. Later on there was a moment of stillness and then, suddenly, motion: like mechanical puppets.

Annaloro scratches in the dark hole of a cupboard. Baboro and his apprentice Alleluia untie the sacks that open wide like mouths, each releasing a puff of flour like a big sigh. Before the front door, armed, still wearing his peaked cap and his short guardsman's cloak, Franzè is moving back and forth, keeping an eye on the rifles and cartridge boxes on the table. All on their feet, including Divinangelo and the child, who are near a still-tied sack. They ignore the woman — or pretend to, now that she's shown her pregnancy. I believe I met her eyes then and they were mocking us.

All of a sudden, we heard the limping walk of Vanzi in the hallway, his rubber soles smacking. He came forward with his crooked gait (it reminded me of the lopsided gait of a wolf). As the commander entered, the boy rushed to tie his shoestrings and then jumped to attention, stretching out his skinny arm.

I represented half of the command, but Vanzi was the one giving orders. He was the politician. In spite of my paramilitary rank, I had no clout: the teacher of little kids. I have always been tall and thin, with knock-kneed legs, a little like a compass, clumsy in my uniform boots, not martial at all.

Vanzi stopped and looked around, ignoring the woman. Someone ordered her to stand up. She laughed and stayed in her seat. But she was staring, staring him insolently right in the face, and she was laughing.

Offended, little Divinangelo screamed, "Have her stand up, make her stand up, or I'll . . ." His bald chin was trembling up and down, his skinny arms were shaking.

"You'll what?" the woman mocked him, "you impotent thing . . . ?"

Vanzi cut the air with his arm, lowered it, and left it hanging. Behind him, the hallway was empty and dark, like an abyss. No one would be able to leave without falling in. That was the moment I felt fear and I sensed that everyone else felt it, too, except maybe the child.

"We will go to the choir stalls," Vanzi ordered dispassionately. "Prepare the lamps."

6. That night remains in my visual memory in flashes. An old man's memory that loses, day by day, the most common words, forgets

the pattern of ordinary habits (but keeps the most remote past intact). When it comes to that night, my memory refuses to remember and I don't even try to overcome it. There is no record of it in my papers, just a date and two words — "War Tribunal"—followed by perplexed exclamation marks. As I recall it and write, it is as if everything were unfolding through unspoken sequences — only noises and, in the end, the child's cry. Maybe as I go ahead, I'll also trace what the voices were saying.

I can see it. The oil lamps — the old ones belonging to the monastery — nightmare of that wretched event. There were not enough, for the entire choir stalls and the flickering flames barely licked the darkness, thick with the atmosphere of a morgue. Like holding a trial with evil spirits hovering, murmured the men later.

Before, during dinner at the refectory, something set us to shivering, and not only because of the cold. The funereal, cloaked prisoner was sitting at one end of the table on the side opposite the door. At the other end, the boy's pale, haggard face, paired with little Divinangelo, both on the same stool. The others were lined up at the left and right sides. And the candlelight flickering off their cheeks, foreheads, yellow noses, Vanzi's deadly pale bald head, the icy, golden flashes of Alleluia's earrings. And fleeting sights of stray, bloodlike streaks remaining from the frescoes on the whitewashed walls. The boiled potatoes, piled up in the plates, had the shape and hue of remnants from an anatomy theater. There was only the mountain fireplace's ravenous hunger, the emptiness of fatigue and agitation. And a sense of unreality, too much like nausea, crept into the body, through what feeds it.

Shortly after, the walk to the choir stalls. Walking in two rows like friars. And the noisy wooden steps of the high predella. Unrecognizable shadows had taken the seats. Next to me are the boy and Divinangelo, sitting in the same stall, both so small, again wedged together. The child gives me a timid smile, like a schoolboy. And right away he lets his head loll, dozing off. He is startled by the blows of the rifle butts, set on the predella on each side, from the first stall to the last at the end of the choir. Those blows are echoing the tom-tom sound of the drum that keeps rolling while he sleeps. In the child's sleep or in my head?

The noises: that pattering of schoolboys at their desks, the creaking of wood hollowed by a million worms, and the dark inarticulate voices resounding in the vault, the echo coming from the vast and abandoned interior, the empty walls. A long nightmare.

And in the end, the child's cry.

II

1. At the usual time, when everybody in the village was scanning the sky, we could hear the dull rumble of the high airplanes. The squeaking little cell doors were slowly opened. At the end of the hallway, next to the prisoner's door, locked from the outside with a bolt taken from the kitchen cabinet, stood Alleluia, his eyes stuck to the wooden door and the red hair on his neck bristling.

"Maybe she had her young," he said.

Used to animals that push through the birthing process by themselves, he believed that was possible in her case as well. Maybe he thought of her as one of those magnificent sows that can push out a dozen piglets, or even two.

"You hear anything?" Franzè asked, his peaked cap pulled down over his eyes.

What can he hear? What did he hear? What's wrong?

The little boy slipped into the group and went on to post his pale bloodless little ear to the door. They couldn't hear a thing. Divinangelo cursed in a whisper. Franzè, in his shirtsleeves, but never letting go of his guardsman's cap and rifle, slapped and tipped his peaked hat. They all wore harsh, tired faces. Annaloro, coming from the kitchen wearing his apron, said he had vaguely heard something at dawn. Again, they all got excited, but it turned out it had been only a dream. Although in fact, she herself, she was the one who said it, right? She was the one who said last night that the time was up, threatening to pop it out there on the floor. They stood whispering, nose to nose, half-naked and numb. Vanzi arrived, limping more than usual, his face dark. The others moved aside and he flung the door open, firmly pulling the latch of the bolt. The woman appeared fully dressed, sitting on the straw mattress, turgid, her belly big under her breasts.

"Well . . . ?" she says. "You should ask for permission before entering a lady's bedroom."

The others left, glumly following Annaloro to the kitchen. With his apron on, he had the reassuring domestic look of a man who lived with plenty of women in his household. Only Franzè, looking dazed, remained on guard duty, with his rifle over his shoulder and his peaked cap high on his forehead.

Guarding "La Rossa." We had caught a red. And we were the blacks, the Neri.

2. The day started off slowly, with the smell of coffee, barley coffee. Meeting in the kitchen, they immediately asked, is she having labor pains?

Since the first morning the boy had taken charge of bringing the hot bowl to the prisoner. Thinking he was responsible for her surveillance, he was the one who pulled the bolt and opened the door to make sure she was still inside. He would leave the door open so he could come back in with an armful of wood and branches. Hers was the largest cell, with a fireplace, probably used in the past as an infirmary. As restless and curious as a pup, the kid went back and forth, smacking the floor with the pigskin soles of his shoes. Below his bare, skinned legs, dropping from his ankles, were the bulging pads of his shrunken wool socks. He was wildly excited, circling the cell, looking through the window bars, spying on the woman, buzzing around her, as fascinated as he would have been by a circus freak. He called her La Rossa, thinking that was her real name.

He was the only one who was always lively and cheerful when he awoke, spurred on by his sense of adventure — it was a big game for him. He was probably eleven or twelve, but his fragile appearance made him look much more childish. Because of his delicate health — he was sick every winter — he could not attend school (besides, it had been closed down by then). His father was teaching him, and the year before the boy had taken an exam; he was extremely shy, but he had a ready tongue. Up there, in the monastery, even scarcely dressed, exposed to the cold and so much stress, he didn't even develop a cough. Since when do men get sick when they are making war? He seemed to confirm that as he ran around day and night, bare-headed. Until they finally gave him that hunter's fur hat, a sort of Cossack's hat that made him look like a gnome and which he refused to take off, even inside. He was risking ringworm, said the woman, laughing. Sometimes she would call him "little wagtail."

The others each made up names for him and only Divinangelo used his name, Erminio, or another nickname he had invented: Nirli. I had often seen him, in the village, sitting next to Divinangelo, the shoemaker, whose workshop was in the rented basement of the boy's house: on the balcony sat the boy's father — an old father — and down by the front door, close to the bench, this skinny child was always busy looking around and chatting.

That was before the fire.

3. I picture him again inside that cell, the door open, putting down the first armful of wood and branches. He learned to pile them up on two stones that served as andirons. He breaks the sticks and looks at her. She does not look at him; silent, large, monumental, she sits unmoving on the edge of the cot.

Through the window bars, a dry, flesh-colored sky, a clear layer of sky, rarified from the drought. He: "At night, you can see plenty of stars up there." The beginning of a conversation, rarely taken up.

"Eh, you," she finally says. "You talk about the stars, you. If it were up to you, I would already be six feet under with a frozen nose."

The boy shrugs his shoulders. "That was fair, woman, those guys have made a mistake."

"Maybe they did," La Rossa admits. "They really have made a mistake." She lets out a throaty laugh.

He has forgotten to keep an eye on her; they are both staring at the flame. Suddenly something tiny and whirling traces a crazy path up the chimney, disintegrating midair in a muffled explosion, a fleeting mineral-blue flash.

"And what was that?"

"The blowfly."

"What kind of blowfly?"

"The bluebottle fly," the woman explains. "He was hiding in the chimney soot through the winter and the fire's spring woke him up, a flame's tongue licked him and he popped like a bubble."

"He made a blue flash," says the kid with a dreamy look.

"A bluebottle," mutters the woman.

And she turns to me — standing still, outside, like a spy — with a look of contempt.

4. She was told to come to the kitchen, only one fire could be fed. She took her time and came, sitting on the bench with her legs open, as she had on the first day.

The men, sleeves rolled up, bustled around Annaloro in his role as cook, except Franzè, who stood guard outside, and the old man, in a corner, wrapped up in his beard and cloak. Vanzi appeared and disappeared, checking that I was keeping to my watch post. He had trusted me with that specific charge, the interest with which I watched over, observed, and, in a sense, spied on her hadn't escaped him.

Yet, at the beginning La Rossa was not completely intractable; she seemed to like company, even though she kept chastising everyone, lashing out right and left with her whip of a tongue. Every now and then she took out the gap-toothed celluloid comb meant to hold her tufted clump of hair and then quickly put it back in, letting the serpentine locks spill out.

"Start talking nonsense, woman," Alleluia invited her, stretched at full length and feeling joyful. His earrings, like a savage's, quivered at his flabby earlobes, dangling like little intestines. He was sitting with the boy, opposite her on the other bench, the two of them waiting as if they were in a theater.

"This yes-man here," she spat on the ashes, "is a little nuts."

And the kid laughed his head off, his neck swelled and the scar turned as red as a wattle.

"You, skinned little snake," she says, "you're in your element, eh?"

Alleluia laughed with his few teeth, sharp, like a wolf's. Everybody laughed.

The woman, as short-tempered as a boy herself, went on with the game, except in those moments when she put on a haughty expression; then she would not talk at all anymore. It happened every time Vanzi stepped in. Usually he stayed in our cell, isolated, setting up a hierarchical distance that I couldn't pull off myself. He came in, glowering, with his limping, sidelong gait; the curls around his bald spot as stiff as wire, his iron eyes half-closed. And he stood there rigid as a statue.

Eh, there is bad blood, the men think, she isn't angry with the kid, but with him . . . he asked for the conviction, kept her on the razor's edge the whole night, is she the kind of woman who wouldn't bear a grudge? They watched them anxiously. I watched them, too, asking myself whether they really saw her as someone to be killed.

Vanzi never said a word to her and she would not show him the whites of her eyes.

15

5. "Did you light the fire with bullets, at the Sallesi's?" Annaloro asks, breaking up some kindling under the cauldron.

A joke like any other, it's not our business to settle scores with the Sallesi, even if they knew of the stranger's trafficking.

"Oh, for sure, she was just carrying the munitions home with her," Franzè replies, lifting up the top of his hat. "But no," he says, "she wasn't going back home. She was walking through the trail of the Incoronata. She was walking along calmly, we crashed into each other at the turn."

"And you," she snaps, "were more scared than I was, handsome fellow."

"We both got scared, and the child you carry startled all the way up to your mouth. You didn't expect any people to be up here, eh?"

"Neither, handsome fellow, did you."

They squabble with no bitterness, as if catching her on the trail of the Incoronata had lost its importance. Maybe they don't even think "what's done is done"; they just want to shun the idea of those others, hiding there, provided that there ever have been any and that there are still a few of them by the Incoronata caves or somewhere else in the mountain. Nevertheless, in the end that thought came to them all. Silence fills the room.

Everybody thinks, well, they are there and we are here, and God forbid that we ever run into each other.

The boy dozes on the bench, leaning on Divinangelo's side, and every now and then he whines and startles himself in his sleep.

6. Of all of them, the only one not sitting near the fire was Baboro the mute, wrapped in his black cloak, with his long beard left unshaven as a sign of mourning.

But he spoke to her, once. He had been staring at her belly for a long time and suddenly asks, "You have had others, eh?" He means children.

And he insists passionately, "Where do you keep them, eh? Where do you keep yours?"

He has buried his son, put him inside four wooden planks; he was the brawniest young man in the neighborhood. (Brawny and dumb—it was well known).

"I have sown them like seeds." But she replies without looking at him, only her tongue is poisoned. "I have sown them around like seeds, exactly like you men do." It's clear she has some respect for the old man; she's talking to the others in this way, though, because they've called her a whore.

At dusk, voices fall. Slowly, the window's square of light above the sink fades away. And the child starts seeing shadows. We all see them. In truth they come forward out of the end of the hallway, crouch hidden in the corners, stop at a certain distance from the fire and can be seen floating in the air and reaching out to us.

Someone asks in a shrill voice for the lights to be turned up. Another takes a piece of kindling, puts it near the flame, then close to the blackened spout of the oil lamp on the fireplace mantel. They look at each other, scrutinize each other, in that flickering light, with a growing sense of panic.

We know, yes, she is here, the woman, and we are all linked by a chain.

III

1. It was morning, late morning, the sun was high. A hobnail step could be heard scraping against the rocks in the churchyard, and little Divinangelo spied out through the window bars. "Goddamn it," he said "a cassock." Franzè peered as well and, as he revealed with a glance, recognized the priest.

They fell silent. Until, with the sound screeching through the whole corridor, the priest opened the door and stuck his head inside. He was a big kid, solidly built, with bright cheeks and eyes as big and brown as a cow's. He seemed astounded by the sight of the woman. And by the sight of the men, with their emaciated faces and the grim look of those who had let their beards grow.

He took off his small round cap with a resounding "May the Lord be praised."

There was no answer.

"I already smell like carrion, apparently," the woman mumbled from her seat.

"As of now, you smell like piss," Alleluia muttered.

The poor priest stood in the middle of the kitchen and turned his head from right to left, not grasping their words or maybe not wanting to believe them. He stopped in front of the woman. Turning his question to everyone, he asked, "Who is she?"

It was the boy, jumping to his feet, who introduced her: "She is a whore."

Franzè intervened: "I know this man. He is the seminarian who helps the priest of Vallepretara parish," and, introducing himself: "I am a guardsman," and he tugged the peak of his hat nervously.

Emboldened, the kid intervened again: "She said there is a stench of carrion."

And Alleluia went on, "She is the one who smells like piss."

The young man blushed, red patches on his cheeks. "Why, folks?" he asked meekly.

Old Baboro, standing up in his cloak that reached to the ground, groaned, "Dogs, have you no manners?"

Some embarrassed laughter followed, and prompt hands pulled up the only straw-stuffed chair, now just about disemboweled. The seminarian put his mountain backpack on the floor and sat down with his little cap on his knees, looking around with his peaceful eyes. They were round, meek eyes, with straight eyelashes, the eyes of a pet. (Even today, after more than forty years, I would recognize him anywhere, if he is still alive and if he was ever more than a ghost.)

"Did you find everything you need?" he started saying with the quiet confidence of a priest in his own house. "I hope the kitchen tools are all there. The straw mattresses are worn out but dry. A few trestles need to be repaired. I see that the fireplace draws well. It's a dry season, but up here it's cold already, soon it will snow. Are you going to stay?"

Silence. Everyone was waiting for the others to talk. They did not look at me, nor did I intervene.

The kid jumped up. "It depends," he said. "Depends on her drum," and pointed his finger at her belly. He gave the coarse laugh he used when imitating the men.

The woman decided to talk.

"You, little priest, take everything in stride. But if you stay here

19

another five minutes, they will break you down. The boy and that fool over there, that savage with the earrings, they both lost it a while ago and practically wallow in it. And all of them are nervous, like sissies. On a different occasion, they would have come and kissed your hand. Now, fear makes them talk nonsense. Their teacher and instructor, this one here, he was born without any guts. Tell them to bring you the other one, Il Nero; he is the politician and leader. If you want to know what I'm doing here, I am waiting to deliver my child so they can execute me. I have no secrets, boys, I tell anybody my business; you, do the best you can."

Vanzi arrived, limping noticeably. With a nod, he led the priest away. He kept him in our cell for a long time. But no one called for me.

2. That night and the next day we didn't hear a thing and the seminarian was still with us. At the table, Baboro and his apprentice Alleluia joined him in the sign of the cross. Though nobody joined the prayer without muttering. His presence was full of the unknown.

But something eventually leaked out. Apparently, he was only passing by; he had come to make sure that the monastery could shelter the new hermit, a pious old man from Civita. Everyone knows that during a war, in a time of massacres, sanctity flourishes as a vocation, as if bloodshed itself feeds it. Nevertheless, the pious old man would have waited for the peak of winter to pass, or better, for late spring, because in the mountains the season always turns harsher, and in any case he'd never have come before he had received news or a message. (Provided that, in the meantime, he did not die or the war ended.) In other words, this one was not going to leave. Priests are curious, as everyone knows, a priest never just takes a look and moves on. Everyone's business is his business. Everybody in the end had already understood that.

On the third day, later in the day, when the woman had already retired to her room and the men lingered around the half-extinguished fire, Vanzi called me and we both went into the kitchen. The seminarian graciously put down his breviary.

"So," Vanzi began without sitting down, "is it true you are not going to Civita after all?"

Indeed, he was not going to Civita nor was he going back to Vallepretara; the parish priest had recovered and did not need him anymore; he was going back home to his village, under the mountain, on the other side.

"Ah, your family," Vanzi says, "when is your family expecting you?"

They didn't know anything, they were not expecting him.

"To get to the point," Vanzi insisted, "can you swear to that?"

He would not swear to it; on the contrary, he was surprised.

"Hey, you listen," Vanzi burst out as he glared around the room. "Here we are already in trouble and we don't want any more. I have already made you a proposal: we trust you, do your inspection of the monastery, and swear on the crucifix you won't breathe a word, and we will let you leave. Try to understand me, I don't want any more complications."

His voice was trailing off, he started finally to realize what the other men already knew from the meek and obstinate expression of the young man, all bones and determination. Well, it's understandable, there is someone sentenced to death, he cannot leave. They expected him to say that, and in fact he did. That was exactly what he said: there is someone sentenced to death and I have to help her.

Vanzi was spying him through the cracks of his closed eyes. "That woman," he burst out, "won't be able to stand the sight of you." But even the tone of his voice was weak.

"I'm staying," the priest confirmed.

"Then so be it," Vanzi said hastily and without looking at him. Aware that his face would show what anyone could see: that he was giving up on convincing the others and controlling what was going on.

I had remained silent. Besides, nobody had said a word to me.

3. The next morning, accompanied by the boy, the young man walked around the monastery as if he were the landlord. He even gave the trestles a shake under the sleepers, to check which beds were unsteady. They worked hard with the hammer, stirring up echoes in the walls. Later on, in the hallway, using a sharp fragment of an ember, they worked together to draw bold numbers over the doors of the occupied cells. From the kitchen a trilling laugh could be heard every now and then and it didn't sound like the kid's usual laugh.

"That man," said Divinangelo, irritated, with his look of a resentful spinster, "is taming him. You know how priests are, they start with the kids."

Cell number one was assigned to the prisoner (the protagonist). The others, on one side or the other, had odd numbers. The kid was totally pleased with the idea. His cell, which he shared with Divinangelo, was adorned with a beautiful, bold number five. Pleased with himself, he pointed out that the place looked like a hotel. The others all went to look. They all liked it; it gave a sense of order and stability. Plus it was creative.

"Logs to room number one," the woman shouted from inside with that petulant tone, typical of her gender, that usually forces every man to obey.

Annaloro rushed forward, his arms loaded with wood. He had a whirlwind of women in his household; they all laughed.

Alleluia was forbidden to use his swineherd's filthy expressions, and he gave the priest his seat, next to the fire, on the second bench. Since they had to stay there, they deeply felt a need to recuperate some sense of normality, to get rid of the sense of making do and somehow settle down. The kid was rebuked for his insolence as well, and, with his tail between his legs, he went over to the cassock. He was already following him around like a puppy.

The woman, so big, and with her own legs wide open, took up the whole bench by herself. The others were scattered around on the kind of three-legged stools shepherds use. Except for Divinangelo, who sulked jealously. He stayed near the table, sitting backward on a little chair made of pale wood. There on the back of the chair you could see a carved inscription — "Panipuccio shepherd" — and the date, recent. Nobody had heard tell of this Panipuccio.

So many shepherds had passed across that side of the mountain and they each had left a souvenir — stools, wooden spoons, a mortar and pestle, even rough crucifixes — in return for hospitality. When the stools were turned upside down, each bore a name and a date. La Rossa claimed the little chair with the back for her room. They let her have it. Baboro, too, spreading his cloak, moved toward the fire and they kindly made room for him. They were packed tightly around the fireplace whenever they gathered there. Only the residents of cell number thirteen, the bosses, eh, stay far from the fire; anyway, they have the German camp stove and two folding cots that don't squeak and the radio and a writing desk full of papers (which they were leery of).

They had not noticed me standing behind their backs, or maybe they were just being provocative. The fact that I had been assigned to surveillance — what's more, without specifying if that meant keeping an eye on the woman — left me alone and suspect. And I was the only one who had refused a weapon.

4. The priest and La Rossa face each other silently. She starts first.

"You, young man, must get it out of your head that I care about your cassock. For me, an old woman, you are still too young to shave. I'm not going to stand on formalities. So, what is your name?"

"They call me the seminarian, as you've heard. Even if I have finished the seminary."

"I want to know the name your mother gave you."

"Antonio."

"Did she call you Tonino?"

"Nino. Now she calls me Don Antonio. Sometimes she says 'Father.' She is a little old lady from the mountains."

He answers quietly, submissively. In that moment, the men like him. Bending over the boy and touching his scars, he skims them delicately, calling him by his first and last name; he knew everything. In the same delicate way he touches the little black stripe that Divinangelo, as the designated father, sewed on the little orphan's sweater. The strip is already frayed, the sweater dirty.

And all of a sudden, the little boy, for the first time, starts talking about the fire. Not in an excited and vulgar way—that artificial tone he usually had, much too self-aware—he speaks well, as he had always heard his father speaking, with a thin voice and his hands gesturing nervously. Minuscule and skinny, just little bones. The other men listen to him silently, looking at his mouth. The woman too, sitting aside, her hands intertwined on her belly, listens.

"I," the child says distractedly, "am running in my shirt and the tongues of flames break through the floor. To lick me. They licked my legs up and down and one has even reached my neck. Here, right here. It licked me like . . . like the bluebottle . . . ."

He had liked the idea of the licking flames and shoots the woman a conspiratorial look. She benignly smiles, as if she were not the one accused of setting the fire.

"And what a bonfire it was!" Franzè intervenes, agitated. "A house full of wood and worms, and the straw beneath." As a guardsman, he was the first to rush there.

The old man's decaying house, filled with antiques, where the solitary man lived with his books and the child. Occupied by Germans. They were staying upstairs in confiscated bedrooms and in the basement was a horse—a young white mare, straight out of a fairy tale, caught who knows where—and, obviously, straw and fodder. But on that night the Germans were not there, nor was the animal.

"And what about my store?" Divinangelo angrily squeaks in the feminine voice of a hired mourner. "My bench, my shoes, my stuff, eh?"

"He, too, lost everything," Franzè admits comprehensively, talking to the seminarian. "All in ashes."

And it was little Divinangelo who had lifted up the scorched child as he clung to him convulsively. From then on, they never separated, though all the women in the village contended for him.

And for the boy it is like finding himself again on that burning floor, his father, already suffocating, not responding anymore. He stirs himself. His throat swells up, he wrinkles his nose and forehead, tickled by his own tears. But he does not weep.

"Tomorrow," the seminarian says, changing the tone, "we will put on some oil. Before you go out you should always grease the scars. The new skin is delicate, it could crack from the cold."

Right. Of course. That's what should be done. Greasing the scars is necessary. They all diligently approve. And with sudden dismay they stare at those miserable skinned little legs as if they were seeing them for the first time. Alleluia, the brute, stretches out a finger and touches them. *Ihii*, he neighs, with his fleshy nose, and his stiff red hair pops up like goose bumps. The seminarian lays his pale hand on that big tufted head as if he were patting the head of a large dog.

A chastened atmosphere drifts through the group. The men give in to a comforting sense of ease; they put themselves, defenseless, in the hands of the young man. Let him judge, let him. A boy, indeed, still thin after the seminary — boys come out of the seminary reduced to skin and bone because of all their study and abstinence, all spirit — a boy who looks in your eyes with a gentle authority. A real do-gooder. And such eyes he has, so sweet and bushy-browed, bovine eyes; saints carry nature within, the good nature of the nativity animals.

La Rossa brusquely stands up, with a small dry laugh. Franzè follows to lock her in, taking up the rifle that for once had been abandoned.

5. The priest was expected to talk to the old man, Baboro. And so he did. But not to Vanzi, nor to me, the presumed leaders. Though I did witness it. Maybe he beckoned for me or maybe I wanted to stay;

in any case, I stayed. Sent out Alleluia, who remained crouched down, the cell door open, the armed man in the hallway, the following day people knew the conversation word for word.

Straightaway, the seminarian said he would not interfere, since he was not allowed to. And Baboro kept silent beneath his beard. He would not interfere; he would keep his word, but he had to assist the woman until the end. (Then I thought: he believed us, he is taking us seriously.)

"You, dear boy," the old man started. But he corrected himself. "You, Father, you do not know. That woman is the devil . . . she is not worth . . . ."

"God will judge her merit. I have to comply with the duties of my office. Only one question: you, as an honest man, loaded with experience, are you sure . . . I mean, according to the martial law you intend to apply, is she guilty?"

"This, too, only God can tell. He is my witness that this is not a vengeance. My son . . . a peaceful boy . . . slaughtered . . . . A country boy, a simpleton, what did he know? He wore the black shirt that does not get dirty and maybe he also liked to show off on Sundays. As for knowing, he knew nothing. Just like the others. We have all been sheep. And so what? But to slaughter him, Christ . . . ."

He was breathless, gasping. I did not intervene; it would have been pointless. The idea of slaughter was nailed into the old man's mind. Actually, it had just been a brawl between muscular, a bit brutal, youngsters, like a fateful fist in the boxing ring. Accidental death, and everybody had come out battered.

He caught his breath. "But it is not for my son that I have said yes, I swear it. On the contrary, I raised my arm for a no, when our leader asked: we shoot her now or wait? Wait, I said, wait until she delivers. The kid, instead, a step ahead of me and the others, was shouting, 'Now, now!' He claims that he saw her in the alley the night his house was set on fire. She denied it, spitting and insulting us. Yet, she was found with her stuffed bundles of kindling. With this woman, we tied a millstone around our necks. She supplied arms to the partisans. She was carrying around the seed of death. Should we let her sow death throughout the area?"

"She does it on one side, you on the other one. Death is sown on this side as well."

"And what to do? It always happens, it's the chain of the devil. I know nothing. I do not know why I came here with these men . . . . What I am doing here . . . . Where I am going. . . . My old wife dragged herself through the yard begging me not to leave. And then she urged her grandsons to go into hiding and join the partisans; that's how women are. But a voice told me: 'Go Baboro, go there.' It was evidently God's will to have me here. And we must kill. We cannot leave her behind or let her go ahead. It is a trap, at this point. Even if I am just an old man, a farmer, the war has wrapped its hands around my neck."

He raised a finger. "Besides, if this was not God's will, then it was the devil's. So what can we do?"

6. The priest's attempts at conversation with the old man must have been repeated; I find traces of them in other papers.

It was the young man who would unexpectedly divert the conversation. All of a sudden, he asks, "Have you thought about the linen?" startling me. And not only me but Baboro, too, already troubled by his own resentments, doubts, scruples. And, too, the man on guard duty in the hallway, and the others, listening with open ears.

"I mean," he continues, unabashed, "some white cloths to wrap up the baby. It could be born in a moment and they won't know what to do. In my sack I have some handkerchiefs. It is a child, an innocent. He comes straight from God's hands."

Baboro piped up: "Passing through that pigsty." But he promptly corrected himself. "Please forgive me, little Father, my dear little priest, in these days I am delirious. But she herself has claimed she followed the Germans to earn a living. She speaks with contempt.

27

Who can understand? But that's what she said. She provokes and bitches. Well, maybe she is the most desperate one. Come on, give me your orders. What was it . . . yes, the linens. And what can we do?"

"Listen, Baboro. I am asking you to take me to her cell now. You and I are going there to sort out this linen problem. And you have to help me, and not only tonight. Talk to the other men. You must let us stay together; let me stay with her in the cell. There is little time left and we need to save her soul."

They were not looking at me, acting as if I did not exist. So Vanzi's order about my presence there was respected. I felt like an exposed spy, but I wouldn't have left for anything. Besides, the speech had been delivered loudly and they all could have heard it. The priest was speaking for everyone.

We moved silently. I gestured at the sentinel to leave. Meanwhile, those two already were at the doorstep and Baboro was knocking. The door stayed open.

The woman was standing erect before the fire. She had thrown her cloak over her naked shoulders. Her large white bosom was visible at the neckline of her homespun shirt. Some cloth, torn into squares, was scattered on the bed.

She said brusquely: "He wants to start converting me now?" The question was addressed to no one.

"Please, listen to him, for God's sake." Emotion cut the old man's breath. "Listen to him, I say. I'm asking you to, woman."

"You? Oh, look who's talking."

"I see that you are already taking care of it," the young man observed quietly and with no hint of embarrassment. "We were just thinking that the child will require some clean linen."

"Here it is, there was no need of you. A large skirt from the village is enough to swaddle ten children. A single skirt from the Sallesi women is worth an entire city layette. Satisfied?"

"When will the baby be born?" the seminarian asked.

She turned her back. "Go away." As she was stretching her hands out to the fire, her cloak slipped down. She had broad white shoulders with two distinct dimples. Baboro made a wry face. Bending down to the ground, the young man picked up the cloak; with a patient naiveté, he turned it a few times in his hands and, figuring out which way it went, placed it correctly over her back.

The woman held it tight around her breast and without looking up, said, "My term is up at the end of the month." She said it firmly; she had understood and wanted him to rest content.

But, after all, it was time for them to know. It was time for everybody to know.

IV

1. In those days, the monastery, embedded in the living rock, was still standing as an imposing single structure; it looked more like a stony bastion than a religious place. Down in front, the open space filled with irregular stone slabs had been the churchyard. In the middle, the long black wrought-iron cross rose up, fixed in a block of stone as white as marble. The little fountain, sending down spring water, was almost hidden on one side, but you could hear its continuous gurgle.

The massive body of the monastery stood at a higher elevation and the way in was through a narrow, steep, tortuous, impracticable flight of steps carved out of the same rock. Even so, before the war, some women, having made a vow, still would climb up there on their knees.

A narrow path surrounded it all and you could also enter the church from the monastery's interior. But the boy's particular feat was to climb all the way up the flight of stairs. During the day he slipped out alone, and sometimes he went quite a distance, ignoring our calls, although at night he could not sleep far from the foul smell and warm shirt of Divinangelo. He would always go back to that flight of steps. More than once I could see him starting up that sliding slope, falling down, trying again, and then yet again the next day.

He puts his foot on the first crumbling step. He looks at his leg in the priest's black sock, his black foot swishing around inside the small pigskin boat he calls a shoe (and that hampers him). He scratches himself. The woolen socks make his new skin itch. And he takes to climbing, wriggling up like a snake. And in the end he succeeds.

On the top, on the stony balcony where the church door opens, he lies clinging to the ground. Maybe he gets caught up by the fear that he could fall and it would be like falling off a cliff, and so he slides back on his bottom toward the doorway.

The day I found myself in the church, I had arrived there from the inside, and with no intention of spying on him, when I heard him coming. He did not see me, although it was not my intention to hide, either. He looked around with a kind of confidence, mechanically making a little genuflection. The cracked walls, the floor with its disconnected slabs, in the middle the ruined low wall of the altar and the choir's semicircle behind: the courtroom. Hands in his pockets, after he makes a hasty sign of the cross before the crumbling altar, he goes and climbs up the central stall, sits down with dangling feet, stretching his little birdlike neck out of his frayed sweater. He is pensive. He stands up, sits down again, gestures, opens and closes his mouth like a fish. Then he is motionless for a long time, his eyes empty, empty as his pale little face and his skin, yellow around the nostrils. A little ghost.

I was sure that he was picturing the climax of the trial, and was seeing the accused against the altar wall as he stared at it intensely. And he was picturing himself as the leader at the center of the choir, making his accusations and disputations all night from the highest stall.

The bitter stench of it still hovered in the air. I myself was taken back to that same moment, when the child, wide awake and as brisk as a sparrow at dawn, had shouted out his condemnation, his thumb pointing to the floor, then climbed down, leaping over Divinangelo's

31

legs and gone to a corner, stretching his legs out near the rifle, to pee.

2. The second time, he spotted me. He was standing straight in that same central stall, on tiptoe. He motioned to me. I did not understand immediately. He wanted to take down a scrolled ornament that hung in a golden frame above the back of the choir stall. Gold shimmered against the dark walnut backdrop and in gothic script: "CHORUS." Written and proclaimed there in a frame, CHORUS reminded him of his father's Latin, the smell of old books, and seasoned wood. It reached out to me as well. I lifted the scroll. He grabbed it.

We went out to the little stony ledge and he childishly stretched a hand to me. The other was holding the CHORUS sign tight against his chest. Alone, he would have thrown himself down to creep along the edge; now he nudged me there, with his tense little arm. Below, across the churchyard, Vanzi was slowly walking. At the low wall he turned, pausing next to the cross, then disappeared out of sight.

All of a sudden, we could hear a drone in the air and the kid lifted his head up like a frightened little animal. Airplanes appeared in the icy blue of the sky, high and unrecognizable, luminous nuclei with silver tails, like comets. They crossed the sky humming and plunged behind the mountain ridges, for a while their silver trails were still visible.

I had felt his cold little hand loosening. Hunkered down, the boy was spying from above. There was the woman at her daily hour of fresh air, wrapped up in her cloak. From above someone might think that she is exactly the same woman who, completely covered in a cloak (like one of the peasants), passed through the street on the night of the fire. Crouching, with a quivering tension in his back, he stared at her. He got on his hands and knees as if he wanted a closer view, to recognize her better.

Now, in the churchyard, the seminarian, one foot resting on the pedestal of the cross, reads through the breviary, keeping it open against his knee. An echo of the stroke of an axe reverberates up from the woods under the slope. Alleluia goes up, hurriedly reaches the low wall, then goes back, always crossing before the woman, but never looking at her. At one point a gleam of light glints on his ears. He is neglecting his guard duty; nobody else is doing it either. The prisoner turns her head to the slope, a trickle of stones falling toward the thick of the wood where the men are gathering firewood, making those axe strokes. The seminarian closes his breviary and stares across at the steep rock wall. There she is; she could flee to the path behind the low wall. And nobody is watching her.

The boy darted and yelled at the top of his voice, *Uhuu*, with such passion he could dry up his lungs. The echo, once the axe strokes ceased, reverberated only with his cry: *uhuu*, a wolf cub's howl. I had to pull him back with force and grab the gold frame before it hurtled down. Immediately Franzè could be seen climbing the slope, hands and feet down amongst the trundling stones, with the rifle knocking against his back, and the seminarian, who was running and waving the skirts of his cassock. They brought her back into the middle without grasping her, as if nothing had happened. And there she was, laughing, freeing her head from the cloth, her serpentine locks in the wind. She was mocking the men, the fierce boy and the thoughtful priest — thoughtful to save her for death. But where in the mountains could she flee in such condition? Maybe she could crawl inside some animal's den to deliver her child like a she-wolf (and she was capable of that). I was struck by the idea of a wolfish nature awakening in all of us.

The wind had risen and was clawing at every face. It penetrated the new skin of the boy's neck and he brought his hand to it. I held him by the shoulders, and he drew close to my side and so we went back through the church. It echoed.

As soon as we walked into the kitchen, he moved away, wriggling as if the contact with me had burned him. He wanted the golden frame and went to hang it in his cell, driving the nail into the wall with strong blows from his hammer.

3. In the morning the monastery was floating. Lapped by a sea of vapors that rose all the way up to the churchyard, it hovered as yellow as an antediluvian skeleton. Horses are swallowed and disappear in it.

Franzè and Alleluia left to pick up supplies from Baboro's farmhouse. When the sky cleared, it was like glass. The wind smelled of coming snow; it swept the air and made the atmosphere crack as if it were breaking. A sky ready to fall to pieces. Instead, around noon, a swirl of tiny fragments came in, the sharp sleet from the mountains. It was the first snow: late, difficult, and bitter. The men gathered next to the woodpile in the kitchen to pass the day. Divinangelo spent hours peeling potatoes. Annaloro pounded the lard, which already was reduced to mush, with gloomy obstinacy. Only children celebrated the snow; ours frolicked across the churchyard.

We calculated that before noon the two men had reached the farm without a hitch, probably without seeing a soul. And no snow further down the plain, only this first sign in the mountains. Anyway, the farmhouse, halfway between the monastery and the village, far away from any other farmhouses, farmsteads, or sheepfolds, was safe and well supplied. There never had been a requisition or a search, the German patrols would enter respectfully, accepting a glass of wine at the most. It was a safe house. The house of the "martyr."

Following Vanzi's order, Franzè, as a guardsman with a safe-conduct pass, would go down to the village to fill us in about the situation. And no chatting with the women. Instead, he was supposed to ask about the women from that area who took to the woods with supplies and weapons . . . the vipers . . . . He had never asked

La Rossa about it during the interrogations, least of all about the Sallesi women who hosted her, and it had been a relief for everybody. Is it ever possible to know what's in a woman's head? So many of them — an epidemic — infatuated with the partisans holed up in the woods. The young ones and strangers too.

"We'll still be here for Christmas," Baboro said, carving away at a white piece of beech. Something for his women, but nobody asked him.

"Well, as for me . . ." Annaloro scratched his ear with a greasy hand. "I would say it has dropped."

"What has dropped?"

"Her belly, I mean. With all these stresses and strains . . . ."

"That woman, goddamn it, is not the type who would have a miscarriage or give birth a single day earlier," Divinangelo muttered, "not even if she were struck by lightning."

"Still, it dropped. It always happened like that to my wife, my first wife. Annaloro, she says, look here, I am about to do it, look."

"Really?" the thin little man inquired, calmly and thoughtfully. He had never been married.

"It's true, I tell you. It starts hanging down, the baby begins heading toward the exit. Look at her, that one is going to give birth soon, I tell you."

"Ok, I'll look at her. They have been in there together for a while. What's he doing? Confessing her? He has guts, the little priest."

The boy came back sprinkled with sleet, his fur hat all aglitter and his pigskin trousers heavy with water. As he slipped off his long black socks and dried his eggplant-colored legs and bloodless little feet, the men kept complaining about their own old and worn-out shoes. If the situation were to take a little longer — and long matters eventually fester — their shoes wouldn't hold up in the mountain snow. They had a single pair of rubber boots among them. Down in the village women and children had been wearing wooden clogs for a long time.

The boy said, "I will make shoes like these for you."

And Annaloro promised to peel whole pigskins away from the lard. They thought about it as they stared at the snaking patterns the flame lapped against the sooty crust of the cauldron.

The boy had fixed it in his mind. The tongues of fire. Hell. Send her there. And may those tongues lick her all over.

4. Usually those two were also there. Quickly, the priest would call back the boy from outside. He led him to the fireplace, checking him over like a mother to see if he had gotten wet, although, after that first sprinkling, it hadn't snowed anymore.

"He needs to stay inside, the cold temperature makes him turn pale."

"He is yellow," the woman points out. "He probably has worms, he looks like someone with worms."

"Bah," Divinangelo says. "When he was home, pampered, he always had a snotty nose and cough. But now he has an executioner's strength. He's jaundiced by nature."

"War," La Rossa proclaims, "weans ahead of time."

"Hehe, do you remember," cackles Annaloro, "how he shouted out: right away? He wanted her to be shot immediately, that's what he wanted."

"War makes even children cruel," the priest murmurs.

"And women," Baboro says "women are like kids, just like kids." And he examines the piece of wood, a side of which is already as round as a spindle.

"Women never grow up," Divinangelo stiffly states. "My late father, God rest his soul, used to say: they get to the mating season and only their wombs mature. Consequently, the growing never reaches their heads. "

"*Ihii*, never grow up" the boy echoes.

"Perhaps," La Rossa says, looking at the priest, "one day they will begin maturing for real and their growth will help the world finally fulfill itself."

"Or perhaps they will remain the world's eternal youth," he kindly replies.

And she retorts, "It is a fact that the revolution is a woman."

Annaloro starts chuckling, maybe picturing, God knows how, the image of such a pregnant and revolutionary woman.

"Goddamn it!" blurted out Divinangelo in his usual irascible manner. "You ever stop to think what you are teaching this here innocent child!"

"You," Baboro answers back, "taught him how to swear."

"Couldn't you say 'What the devil?'" the priest suggests.

And the little man seems struck by this. "What the devil," he ponders. "What the devil," louder. It seems to sound just as good as the other expression.

At the table, Vanzi nibbles with a haughty expression, resting his cheek on his fist, sitting crookedly; only his thick eyebrows and the slits of his eyes, flashing now and then, can be seen. He has always been a violent man, and even weakened by that leg, he doesn't give up. A brute exposing himself to danger, ready for any war. Always arrogant and agitated, he had never been seen in the village without a uniform. The others dart rancorous glances at him, convinced he is the one to blame for everything: the spreading hatred, the revenges and reprisals, the need to exile themselves. And maybe it wasn't even necessary. He wanted all this so he could enter the fray again with his crippled leg. And now he has to put up with a woman, in other words, a tangle of snakes. Here we are in deep trouble. And what are we going to do now? After taking his last bite, he glances around like a basilisk, gives orders, and leaves.

But there will not be any guard duty outside. The one who has been handed the assignment protests he won't go out and freeze his guts. And no more night guards either. The dangers, the men claim, are all in Vanzi's deluded mind.

Whispering, they have started calling him "Il Nero," like the woman does.

5. A day like many others. Some sleet in the morning, whirling and thickening snow around noon, and again sleet, as dry and prickly as chaff.

The prisoner was in the kitchen, there was no need for a guard in the hallway. The young man stayed there as well. He read his breviary, leaning against the table, now and then glancing at her. The boy, curled up like a cat, finally fell asleep on the bench. The men silently stared at the belly that entirely occupied their thoughts.

At dusk, after they had taken turns peering outside, someone said out loud what they all feared: if the snow continued, the others would be stuck at the farm. And the supplies were almost gone. Grunts followed. Baboro silently spun the white spindle with his ancient wrinkled fingers.

"My wife had better send me some tobacco," Annaloro burst out, "or she will be in trouble when she sees me."

"Maybe she will see you again," Divinangelo sharply insinuated. "The devil knows if we are going to save our skin." He had become fond of the devil.

"Only God knows," the priest corrected.

And Annaloro, a second later: "Down with the astrologer!"

The boy woke up and laughed; everybody laughed.

"The astrologer," Divinangelo explained, "that's me."

But they did not talk anymore. A torpor weighing down and slowing their bodies kept them leaning toward the flame. Every now and then the woman stirs her sore body ("a woman and a fire have to be stirred every once in a while"), lifting up her breasts to relieve her belly, shaking her skirt and adjusting it over her reddened legs. Her skirt gives off a smell that the men, maybe even the young man in a cassock, can recognize. For the men it is the smell of women, of their wives as well: homely, a bit depressing, the smell of women when they haven't washed or can't be touched because they're too far along in their pregnancy. But the boy felt a nauseating and at the same time perturbing sensation. He was reluctantly sucking a crust of hardened bread and then, all at once, he threw up.

The seminarian wiped the boy's mouth with his handkerchief. He handily turned the vomit into the ashes with the shovel. It's nothing, just sitting there for hours bent over your stomach and a too-dry piece of bread. The boy felt the acid taste rising in his mouth, he twisted his lips.

It was time for everybody to purge themselves a bit. Franzè had been ordered to bring a paper bag of Epsom salts. They all needed to wash their tongues.

6. It got worse at night. They were about to retire to bed when the woman called out in her commanding tone, almost shouting. Only the boy stayed asleep on the bench and didn't wake. Vanzi had rushed in as well. Once the latch was released, the thick pregnant face appeared under the halo of the oil lamp that hung from a wooden peg. She was not lying down, but sitting on the straight-back chair. She was wheezing, her chin lifted, moving the weak halo of the little flame in the air.

She said: "He wants to confess me? Well, then let him confess me, I am here." She was talking and looking around as if she intended to do it publicly. "Eh, he dragged me to it. He wants me to spill the beans? I will. But he will have to hold his nose."

She was laughing without opening her lips, jolting her whole body. All that bloated and ripe flesh and there he was with his cold steady expression like the effigy of a saint. He doesn't speak: he is thinking.

The men were waiting. The seminarian has received his orders: you will have your flock of sheep—souls inside their fleeces, everyone knows—and your neighbors, all are souls. An idea that, at the moment, seems stereotypical and abstract. Yet here so solid and sinful. Even so, he will know how to figure it out. Christ, why isn't he talking? Sure, if you run into a crazy sheep—and with a fleece so thick that only a pike could run it through–maybe seminary studies are not enough, you should be a thaumaturge and use touch. Let him touch her, c'mon, touch her. They were staring at him, dismayed and almost issuing a threat: don't let him lose to her, don't let that demon of a woman beat him.

But instead of answering the woman's provocations, the priest, in a humble tone, addressed the men. "My father always taught me: human flesh is not a hunk of pork, it contains the soul. He was a shepherd, my father, he used to pasture the flock in the mountains and meditate." He smiled with an open expression on his face.

Again, he had disappointed them. Someone who has gone to seminary, oh c'mon, his father was one of us. What an oracle. They were staring at him and could not understand why he had gone all the way back to his origins, as if he had never taken the plunge away from the ditch of ignorance. There he was, inexperienced and quiet.

He says, "Every moment is the right moment to speak out, eh, fellows? Let her speak, if she wants to. We are here, we can listen to her, why not? Speaking up always does a person good."

He seems happy, we're not sure why. Well, let him hold his nose now; he wanted it.

Nothing scandalous happened. On the contrary, that was the night the weird story of the eye in a stick began.

V

1. A week had passed. Franzè and Alleluia arrived at noon, pushing the mule with its fully loaded packsaddle over a crackling crust of hard frost, their beards stiff with cold around their dry lips. The air was a transparent sphere. The snow had stopped.

From behind the window bars, the others cried out in joy and went out to greet them, all of them red in the face, steaming like mules themselves. In the kitchen, they unloaded the large bags of flour and potatoes first, then the individual packets and bundles sent by the women were handed out to each one. The kid hopped around, crazy with pure curiosity. And he tore into several of the packets, starting to rummage through them, and got a few friendly slaps in return.

"Whatever's shut asks to be pried open," the woman said.

They looked at her resentfully. She's already here and starts to play the sibyl again.

The seminarian joked, "We cannot give you the purge." He was preparing a large cup of it for the boy.

Jaundiced to the whites of his eyes, Vanzi opened his envelope, tearing it apart. With his brother, he was in charge of the post office, and the brother had stayed in the village to run the place. He had been sent some papers that he immediately put back into the envelope. That surprised me. We had no news; our radio was broken

41

and by then useless. The last message we picked up was "Snow has fallen on the mountains." He had passed it on to me while I was writing in the middle of the night. After that, silence.

Raising an eyebrow and slyly winking, he gave Franzè permission to talk in front of everyone. Franzè got the hint and hastily gave a report. Our village was still quiet. News of roundups and reprisals had come from other districts; even nearby, two shepherds had been executed for knocking down and disarming—but not slaying—a German soldier caught stealing a suckling calf. Nothing had happened in our neighborhood, even the women stayed secluded. He swore he had kept the secret even with his wife. He had left Alleluia at the farm to slaughter a pig. Two, actually. As a skilled pig butcher, he had done a good job and now they were carrying fresh meat and sausages. In order to prove it, Alleluia dangled pieces of bloody pulp and unfolded pink necklaces made of sausage, getting everyone's attention.

As for Franzè, he had presented himself, as agreed, to the Kommandantur. The passes were in order, stamped and restamped; a safe passage for all of us. No special instructions, at least so far as he could tell. Obviously, keep our eyes open, do surveillance, search the area (who would want to go further than the woods to gather firewood, anyway?), report any suspicious movements. Anyone spotted or captured? "Nary a man," he has assured the Germans. It's the truth, right? (As for the priest, he didn't come under the category of either man or woman.)

"None of us," Baboro said, "wants to meet someone from the village up here and shoot."

"Or get shot," grunted Divinangelo.

"At least this is not what we wanted, God is our witness."

"But maybe this is what we will get, if we continue to stay up here."

Franzè thought a visit was likely. Construction projects for a cableway at the Rapina were being organized; someone, sooner or later, would stop there. If they were going to hide the woman, they had to keep their eyes open.

The woman jumped up. "You care, eh? You want to be the ones to kill me."

"Would you rather," Franzè fired back, "be handed over to the Germans?" And then suddenly lost his temper. "I can make the suggestion myself."

"Nobody would accept such a proposal," Baboro replied indignantly.

And Franzè shouted: "I make the suggestion, I make it now. And you, old man, you also raised your arm to vote to save her."

"Not to save her," Baboro solemnly replied "but to save her child. We have to wait, it's decided. I refuse to hand her over."

"Eh, eh," La Rossa started to snigger. "The child, eh, they pass the buck. Your good conscience is anxious for the innocent. You have captured me, kill me then. Go ahead, hand me over to the Germans. They do not make a fuss, those people. They kill quickly. I want you to hurry up." She was shouting now. "C'mon, riddle me right away. You have to shoot here, make a sieve of this whore's belly with everything that's inside it. Man's semen, ha-ha. I'd like to use my nails to tear out this fruit of your filthy race of male hypocrites." She was crumpling her skirt, panting as if her belly were fatally weighing her down.

The seminarian had tried to take away the kid, but he put his foot down stubbornly and wouldn't move, so he pressed him against his cassock, putting his hands over his ears. It didn't cross their minds to order her back to her cell, although Vanzi warned she should stop cursing and provoking them. They were all thinking about the coming labor, astounded. God forbid she has a miscarriage under their eyes, eh, no, why hurry now?

It was nothing, just one of her raging outbursts, a way of defending herself by going on the attack. An extraordinary woman. An explosion of female rage always freezes a man's guts. The Germans themselves would rather have nothing to do with a fury like that.

And meanwhile, the festive atmosphere had been spoiled, and they sat with their packages on their knees, feeling bitter. I had also received a package, sent from Z. I hadn't expected it and didn't open it in front of the others. It was extraordinary the way women could always find everything, tobacco too. Even cotton, gauze, and disinfectant inside the package that disappointed the little one. In mine, from Z., two reams of paper and ink for my fountain pen.

They started in once again, unfolding the packages, and took out some little cookies. It was Annaloro who offered her an anise *ciambellina* to win her favor. He loved fat women, the kind of large woman who so peacefully can fill a thin man's house.

She accepted the *ciambellina* and started gnawing on it.

2. Late in the night, in the total silence when everyone was asleep (the radio that carried the forbidden stations he secretly listened to now dead), Vanzi summoned Franzè. I noticed the way he glanced as he came into the room at the papers scattered on the rickety little worm-eaten table that was used as a desk. As if he were afraid of having to undergo a formal interrogation — one written down in black and white.

He confirmed that the village was quiet. Apparently — he added after a brief hesitation. Sufficiently quiet for the Germans to not harbor suspicions or act cruelly. The women, though, had gone on with their clandestine trafficking. They claimed they were going to get some firewood, wadding the supplies under their coats, and came back from the woods with slim bundles of sticks on their heads. Fugitives also arrived from the city; first they were hidden, then they crossed the lines, led through the mountains by old shepherds and sometimes even by one of the more reckless girls. (In our village nobody ever squealed, on either side).

Welcomed inside the houses, tamed by the cozy warmth and the wine, the Germans would sit next to the fire without any suspicion, and sometimes they slipped off their belts with the machine guns, putting them down to show the women pictures of their own children. They petted the village children and brought canned food and sweets. And maybe, just under their feet, somebody was hiding. The women were above, wearing smiles.

How our position was viewed in the village wasn't easy to grasp. Franzè uttered the word: collaborationists. The "blacks" uniformed and armed at the service of the Germans. No, none of our neighbors. Besides, the young had all disappeared. Every once in a while, there would be an unexpected roundup. Aiming their machine guns, the Germans dragged the elderly out of the houses and took them to dig in the snow. No reason, only to make an example of them. As for the cableway at the Rapina, everything was said to be halted. It seemed that things at the front were not going well. This last news, strictly classified, was sent by Vanzi's brother, the temporary postmaster, and it was not written down on the papers in the envelope.

So were we considered collaborationists? Franzè didn't think so. After Baborino's death and the fire, the cautious thing to do, a way of getting out of the fray, was going away to avoid frictions and complications, both with the Germans and the people. "A trip to the country, eh?" someone insinuated. Or, "Do you want to be hermits?" The women recommended they nurture the little orphan, keeping him warm. A bit of bonhomie and a bit of mockery. We were not black brigades, we were not an advanced patrol. We were nothing. Maybe a sort of no-man's-land between the two fronts. A safeguard.

But for heaven's sake, never talk about our prisoner! On this point, Vanzi insisted strongly. She had disappeared, and people thought she had moved back to the city. She was a tramp and an adventuress who had left the same way she came. Neither Franzè to his wife nor Alleluia to Baboro's Baba had uttered a single word. Instead, the women, old and young, were talking, all bustling around.

45

It seemed as if they had not troubled to keep their secrets, or they did not really fear any reaction on our side. Husbands, brothers, sons, innocent even if they were compromised: the women wanted them all back safe and sound.

Finally, Franzè muttered something about a mystery at the farmhouse. He mumbled between his teeth: "the Moors." Vanzi lost his patience. Franzè came out with it: "Baba was hiding strangers." "What strangers?" It was Alleluia who had found out about it, by chance. He got it into his head to take back the old pig gelder's stick that he used when he would go round the nearby villages with his scalpel-like knives, the bloody small intestines hanging from the stick's tip. (His banner, his blazon, before he retreated to the sedentary job at the farm.) He went looking for it in the underground space behind the cellar, a sort of cave where scrap, old tools, barrels with loose staves, iron fragments and bits of corrugated steel were all piled up; in short, all the useless junk that in a farmer's house is never thrown away. But the entrance to the cave, a hole, was blocked by scaffolding loaded with bottles, flasks, and jars. And behind it, planks he'd never seen before were put up. Alleluia peeps through the cracks, moving aside a straw panel. There, in the cave, are people. Strange people. Dark. Men, women, children, so immobilized and flattened that they seemed to him like frescoes painted on the church walls. That's what Alleluia had confided to him.

The same day Baba calls them aside and orders them never to go down there again and never to talk about it with anyone, not in the village and not at the monastery, absolutely not to share a word with that "ringleader." Old Baba's authority had struck a reverential awe in the apprentice, and even Franzè himself was frightened. But ultimately he had an obligation to report it to his commander.

He was asked to repeat the description of those "Moors" as he had heard it from Alleluia. They were all draped in black, like mourners, the women plump with pitch-black curly hair, as well as two young girls, all with curls, too, and the men, small and thin, very dark, with beaked noses.

Vanzi looked askance at me. "Jews," he muttered between his teeth.

I was relieved to think of them there, safe in the house of the "martyr."

3. One night, while everybody was dozing in front of the fireplace, sated and pacified by the pleasant smell of tobacco and fried meat, the woman quietly resumed her talk about the eye in a stick.

It was about a certain dream. Apparently this dream (or was it a daydream?) had been haunting her since she was young. She thought she was inside a stick, trapped there in the wood with an eye on top. In the dream, with her one eye, she could inexplicably see herself, see the desperate expression of her captivity. Maybe, she says, it lasted only an instant, but she felt as if she had suffered that torture all night long. In a word, she had suffered horribly from her condition. Which one? Well, to have an eye open at the top of the most profound helplessness, to be an eye in a stick. Hard to understand? Indeed, she herself had fought that condition—ignorance—like a prisoner in chains.

Listen to her, somebody says. She had started speaking properly, all of a sudden, as it used to happen to the boy, like a teacher or a priest. She is educated, they comment, in the city there is more education.

"Now you would like to know," she continued with a suddenly embittered voice, "where I come from and who I am. Otherwise, you think, what is she talking for?"

"You can tell us, why not?" the kid intervened, completely shaking off his sleepiness.

"Here he is, he would like to know that, uh? He would like to hear me confess that I have been sent from the city to organize the resistance, that I've provided weapons and killed and set fires, all by myself. This is what you all would like to know, eh? But I repeat that I came upon the mule with the rifles while I was out for a walk. And that I came to this place to make a living off the Germans. Is that ok?"

The boy said, "Right, they wanted to play your drum, that's what they wanted." And instinctively he hunched his head, shielding himself with his arm.

He made her laugh. "He is your little monkey." Calmed again, she started talking about where she was born. A block at the outskirts of the city, those blocks of slums like desolate ghettos where the most impossible people are sent, the always-hungry mob, barefoot, naked, and ready to riot. Those were her people. She says she'd much rather have been born in the countryside. "Everybody should be born in the countryside. Even if the children run around barefoot, it is different. And they kill the pig," she added, recovering her harsh tone.

"But in the city," Baboro observed, "there is more education. I only know how to make the sign of the cross."

"There, people like us get just enough education so we can be crucified. To this day, maybe, after chewing so much printed paper, am I sure I have my spelling and my verbs straight? In school I had to learn a new language, one we didn't speak in our tenements. I couldn't enter into that language. The teacher herself would get discouraged; in her opinion I was inarticulate. Like an animal." She was pensive.

"And you," she brusquely addressed me, "what have you done, you, mister teacher, you have managed to close the one eye they have."

It was a low blow that winded me.

"Then I had to work as a servant," she began again with a menacing calm. "In the houses, I used to steal. It was a fixation, I would steal newspapers, magazines, and books. I barely understood half of what I read there, always craving to know, I felt as if I were blind and mute. I stopped being a servant but I have always worked — real work, manual labor. And I have studied as much as I could."

48

"A man," Divinangelo says, pensively, "is always craving, we know that. A man is an insatiable animal. Me, for fourth and fifth grade, I would walk eight kilometers every day. I thrust my legs into the snow up to my knees, blowing on my fingers and urging myself on: I must make it, I must do it. And I made it. I got a nice yellowish certificate with blue doodles."

"And were you satisfied?"

"Of course I was, sure."

"I still dream," the woman says, "that I am an eye in a stick."

And the boy: "You dream you are an eye in a rifle's sight."

He got up, stretching himself, went to climb up on the sink and, pressing his nose against the dirty window glass, announced, "The stars."

4. Vanzi confronted the priest while everyone was there. They were all going to bed as usual when he turned with sudden determination, looking around for support. He implored the priest, since he was there and he wanted to stay, to get involved, even better, to give some advice. Isn't it true, folks? Let's have him advise us, since we can't come to an agreement. Nobody opposed that.

"Bring back the woman," he replied promptly. "Go back. Nothing irremediable has happened. Stay in your house, in your village. Everything will be fixed. It is a mountain village, people are peaceful. And she, with a baby . . . . Anyway you will keep an eye on her."

He was looking around quietly, catching a glimpse of relief in their tense faces. Ah, a way out of the trap!

But Vanzi didn't hesitate. "You, you are making a blunder. We left, and they won't forgive us for that."

The woman said, "You're on your own like scabby dogs."

"Ok then, we're on our own like scabby dogs. In the mountains, hatred is stubborn. This is how it is and there's no way out. Who will be next? Whose house will be torched? Who will be massacred like Baborino? Who will be beaten, knocked down, like the German soldier? Or shot? This is what is waiting for us if we go back now."

The woman said, "Hatred has been sown here for more than twenty years."

"Others had sown it before."

"Right," Annaloro groaned. "Who started it? That's the trouble. We never know who started it." Twenty years before, as an arrogant thug, he had picked up a truncheon, too. Christ, had those people forgotten? It's all one chain.

Franzè turned to Vanzi, narrowing his eyes. "Give us orders," he burst out. "You've been . . . I mean . . . I've followed you to the line of fire. You gave the orders and I would throw myself forward. Me and plenty of others. Do you remember that? Why don't you want to command us anymore?"

"In war . . ." Vanzi was looking at him in bewilderment. "In war? It was another thing, Franzè, another thing." The weak voice he had when he was discouraged. At least two of those men knew that voice.

"This is war too, for God's sake. Even worse. And you know perfectly well that we should have searched the area and flushed them out, immediately flushed them out. That we should have organized an expedition against the Sallesi. But at least this one has fallen into our arms . . . If we leave her now she will be the first to start again . . . The baby, well, it's all nonsense. She is not the type to spend her time cuddling a child. We cannot leave her behind. We need to bring her in, chained to our feet dead or alive. And alive, it's not possible."

The woman said, "You'll drag me along, dead at your foot, Nero. Heavy, dead, at your crippled foot. You will not go far."

So, now she is bringing us to trial? A murmur ran through the room. And Vanzi, in a voice deprived of all authority: Make her quiet. Silence fell.

50

Wriggling free of the priest, who was trying to hold him, the kid brazenly placed himself in front of the men.

"We had a trial, no? So why now . . . . Don't let her go. It was for real, wasn't it?"

The boy is right. What? Start all over again? He is right. The men grumbled with stubborn faces, like boys making their claim in a game. They hadn't wanted to go along with Vanzi.

"Then," the seminarian observed, "we are back to the start."

"With you, too," the men replied, hating him for meddling, even though they had asked him to. No, he must stay out of it. Feeling their blood run cold, in vain, ah no, not that. They don't even listen to him when he asks Vanzi for formal permission to be granted a few hours to lend his spiritual assistance to the prisoner in her cell. Let the priest and Vanzi come to an agreement. Do the priest and the condemned woman need some privacy? OK, they can have it.

To tell the truth, they were getting too used to living together.

5. The great snow, plentiful and peaceful, which protects the seeds beneath the earth and the first green shoots of grain, was delayed by sleet and stiff winds from the north. They feared its coming. They rarely went out. Only the boy and Alleluia would run around without a care.

In cell number one there was the iron cot with the best straw mattress — even if it was lumpy like the others — military-issue gray blankets and the only pillow, made of wool. On the days the priest spent a long time there, they did not scrimp on wood — they burned up half the woods. The walls became so parched that the plaster peeled off in crusts that looked like scabs. In front of the fire, she kept Panipuccio the shepherd's little chair, with its tall, narrow back that towered like a throne. The priest would bring in one of the three-legged stools with heart-shaped seats for himself. To rule out the semblance of a confession, the woman called for me and always left the door open. I stood by the threshold. Whoever was passing by glanced at us. Besides, her loud voice could be heard distinctly, like a preacher's.

From the milking stool the young man looked at her with a domestic animal's steady patience and sense of quiet expectation. Every now and then her heavy breathing could be heard, the panting of her large, oppressed body, her throat clearing, belching. She muttered, "It is you who wanted this," and laughed. But it wasn't right to stay there and spy on her, a woman in such condition. Sometimes he got called away. On one occasion she kicked him out, but he stayed by the door; when she opened it again she was holding the full chamber pot. He took it from her and went to empty it himself.

But she talked. After the boy brought her the morning meal and the wood for the fire — they treated each other nicely then and she called him little wagtail — she looked better. She had dipped some biscuits in her breakfast bowl, straightened the blankets, and taken her place on the little chair. As for the priest, hunched on the three-legged stool, he seemed to be squatting there. He would ask, "Are you feeling better?" At that time of day it was going better, she was in a better mood.

Once she mentioned the notebook. "In case I have to entrust it to you. I . . . I write." (She looked at me.) "I keep it under the mattress. I had it on me when that boor caught me. I have always carried it with me. You're not laughing? Maybe I . . . Maybe you really are making fun of me." And she was the first to laugh at herself, her face thickened with a repressed and melancholy laugh. "Expressing one's self, what a great thing. But me . . . an eye in a stick."

All of a sudden, she lost her temper. "You want to make me talk, eh? And here I am with my mouth open. But it is plain that you are not here pointing at me like a hunting dog just to have a chat. You are like those there in the kitchen who would like to hear me say that such and such a political faction ordered me to do this and that, that I have shot, set fire, and so forth. If this is the confession you are after, you might as well leave. Sure, I am neither on their side nor yours. Right, but you, on whose side are you?"

Another time she attacked him about the notion of sin. She recalled the time she was a girl in the tenements. A precocious child, all the children there were precocious, they saw and immediately knew everything. "Precocious but not a dupe. I fell for a limping boy who used to come on his crutches to play. He was my first love." A quiet giggle.

And then the mean reproach. "What upsets a woman is obviously deep in her guts, we are not superficial like you. Here people know that. No, we would not talk about it at the Sallesi's, with those women you cannot have certain conversations (and neither could you have an abortion). I say that here people call shame the male sex and nature the female one. It says it all. Our sex is deep and fertile like nature. Well, I was that girl whose soul was in turmoil because of a limping boy. You have probably concluded that I was already loaded with sins. And maybe you even know very well that sin in itself does not really exist. You invented it. And threw it on women. The body of sin. I was full of it up to my eyes. OK?   ' Of course I turned into an ugly girl, and smart to boot, completely unlikable. Then I learned how to take advantage of that. He was a good-looking man, let me tell you. No, that's enough. I spit on him. Anyway, a man is always in heat, but if a woman likes it, too, she's a whore."

Other times she started with a provocative burst of laughter, looking at the young priest, who was filled with compunction as if he really were receiving a confession. And she would come up with one of her absurdities.

"I laugh, yes, about a thought that just came to my mind. And why shouldn't I say it, I don't feel uneasy at all. Here: by way of cheating nature, we might as well end up deceiving her completely. Ha-ha, what a good joke for the Almighty: escape from his power completely. Getting used to, let's say, preferring one's own sex or even oneself. What an enormous joke: the overpopulated and over-coupled world, reduced to sterility. Ha-ha, to remain alone even in love. Well, why you are giving me that look? Are you maybe thinking that I do it? Sure, dear, I really feel like titillating myself with my womb swollen like a toad. How about you? These are boarding school things, eh? You know them, eh? No, I won't stop. I want to talk and talk nonsense as much as I like. And you have to listen to me, or there's nothing. Otherwise I don't confess. Deal? But now get out of here. Go, go away."

Those days she made everyone's head spin. She preached to the audience. If she was feeling calmer, she attacked in a mocking tone.

"Alright, I will use the formal address with you. But do not believe that I consider you to be someone with the power to absolve me. This is why we have a witness here, our assiduous schoolteacher. But I might as well start calling you a helpless novice if I feel like it. I talk and talk. Evidently I really will have to die, never in my life before have I talked so much. It is like when a dying man takes off his clothes. You know that, no? They flounder about with their hands trying to take off their clothes, they uncover themselves, shedding their junk in order to take leave of this world. This is man. And I, I am taking off my own skin.

"But are these idiots really going to kill me?"

6. Rubbing some oil on his neck then burrowing under his fur cap, the boy goes out by himself, and no one opens an eye as they sit drowsily by the fire. Outside in the icy and sunny air, he breathes with his mouth open, puffs, parts his legs, and pulls up his pants, adjusting his crotch as he's seen the men do. He feels like a man. Goes back and forth, whistles and puffs more air. A brave breath comes out of his mouth and nostrils. He is like a colt. He trots a little, kicks, rears up, maybe picturing an arrogant fool who would like to saddle him.

Emerging from behind the low wall: the sentinel. Although he appreciates the exciting taste of performing for someone, when he wants to be alone the boy is suspicious. As for me, he pretended not to see me. He turns on his heel and starts to climb. The steps are like glass. His shoes over his shoulder, he has to climb on his hands and feet like a little monkey. By now he feels confident. Once he has reached the top on his hands and knees, he stays close to the ground for a while. He turns over to lie on his back and be sucked in by the sky. If some airplanes pass, the sky is an upside down sea with shoals of silver fish. When he rises up again he must be freezing. Standing still, he furiously caracoles, shakes his arms, growls a little, pretends to give himself a scare. And then he runs inside the church.

I spied on the boy out of acute curiosity and because I could identify with him. Although my childhood had only imaginary adventures, executed under the jealous and exclusive protection of my widowed mother, I could see myself in him. When La Rossa had said: he is doomed to masturbation—I had relived an anxious moment, in the distance now, but hardly faded. My mother's friend, a real busybody and quick to judge, would look at me and use the same word. It puzzled me. To masturbate: a word obscurely shameful. If it means to pick one's nose, search, and bring into the mouth . . . no, she could not see me. If she meant . . . impossible, a woman is made in a different way, she cannot know this. But if it meant that I will always be afraid of the dark . . . afraid . . . everybody is afraid, men too, it's enough to hide it. If only I could fall asleep and overcome the temptation to slip into my mother's bed and lie next to her . . . ah, they would see. The solitary excitements.

The morning when the boy rushed in, sliding down the glass flight of steps, he had seen bears. He screamed, "Polar bears!" And two big white bodies were advancing with little Divinangelo and his small rifle in the middle. They were Germans in camouflage uniforms. It meant that there was a blanket of snow at the Rapina. The boy then immediately recognized Hans and Fichter and ran up to them to hug his friends' knees.

When they left Vanzi's room, they stayed for a while by the fire in the kitchen. The woman had been locked in. Annaloro prepared a pot with his herbal infusion. They liked it: Hans was affectionately slapping the boy on his back, he touched the little black rag on the sweater and shook his head. He had uncovered his blond head, his short curly hair stuck up. The other, frowning, was looking around, his eyes half-closed and spying. They talked to each other in German while the others just stared at their mouths. The boy clearly liked listening to them. He could understand a little; Hans apparently used to talk to his father, in Latin also, and they played music together. He was staring at him, enchanted, maybe reenvisioning him shaking the violin in his arms with his blond head like one of the big angels from the paintings. His father at the piano. A smell of dust and staleness, old, the smell of his house.

Then everything burned down. War does not let even the smell of the world remain. Everywhere is like this, the whole earth a bonfire. Hans (if only he understood), do you find this bonfire warm? He does not understand, he nods his head, comically rejoicing, pulling chocolate and cigarettes out of his pockets. The men felt certain that those two would never again return to the warmth of their own hearths.

VI

1. The bagpipers suddenly began to play in the churchyard. A rending rip ran through the broad silence of the mountains, slashing into it with a sustained sequence of ragged sounds that gradually ended on a feeble note. The effect was only a little less than an explosion. Startled, the men ran outside.

There were two of them, two bearded shepherds in thigh pads, gaiters, and sheepskin vests. With their ruffled hair, swollen cheeks, and narrowed eyes, they were staring and puffing out the Christmas carol "You Came a Star from Heaven" on their pipes.

They were led inside while Vanzi, with his scathing basilisk eye, was searching for whoever was supposed to be on guard duty at the low wall. He took a seat in the kitchen — something he rarely did — taking a spot on the bench next to Baboro, who had been sitting there, coughing, for quite a while. A few minutes later, at Vanzi's nod, the click of the bolt: the woman was locked in. The seminarian too had been taken to his cell and warned not to show up. Franzè came back without his rifle.

The little boy and Alleluia had crouched down near the mighty legs wrapped in fleece to stare at the instruments. The two shepherds were sitting stiffly across from Vanzi and Baboro on the other bench, looking beyond the men's heads, with blank looks on their faces. The typical attitude of a shepherd who finds himself again among people, patiently waiting to be brought back and drawn into the common circle.

They were from Brecciarola, a village of farmhouses and farmyards spread across the other side of the mountain. Vanzi questioned them at length. The cannon's roar had been heard there, rolling like thunder in the distance by day and like carts on the village cobblestones by night. They knew nothing, but—people say—the war is at a standstill at the coast. With the arrival of the north wind and blinding sleet the airplanes had disappeared. The war has stopped.

"And you," Vanzi says, "where are you heading?"

They were going down to the villages for the Christmas novena. There was nothing strange about it, the pipers always come down to the valley to play under the houses and in the churches, standing in front of the Nativity scenes. Christ is born even in these days. And why had they happened to blow their instruments in the churchyard? Did they know so-and-so from Brecciarola?

It turned out that they knew everybody, like real *brecciarolesi*, and they were obviously passing through Acquafredda because the monastery offered shelter during the hours of the curfew. They had played in the churchyard because the smoke coming out of the chimney sent out a sign of life. It was all completely reassuring. If only the older one were not furtively looking around. They suspected he was looking for the woman.

They all looked at Vanzi. He was tense, his eyelids lowered, frowning. No question he immediately had that suspicion. As the shepherds were putting down their instruments, all eyes were on their chests and waists. They didn't seem to be armed; no need to search. But what about their saddlebags? They took out a wrinkled wheel of pecorino cheese, two little baskets of fresh ricotta; they had a flask of wine, the sparkling, sharp, light wine of our stony ground and also some Centerbe, the aromatic liqueur so strong it could resurrect the dead. Such a varied feast was cheering, and alcohol loosened even the silent shepherd's tongue.

That same shepherd, once Vanzi retired, asked what they were doing up there. Franzè replied, "We are passing through." And the other shepherd: "Are you going far?" Franzè, vaguely: "Soon we will be back on our way." "The north wind is blowing through the mountains so hard that it burns the devil's beard. Is he coming as well?" The shepherd pointed to Baboro, whose breathing was labored as he dozed off.

"Him as well, why not?" the short-tempered Divinangelo answered resentfully. "We are all strong. Eighty-year-old men can take a girl and even get her pregnant. They make war too."

Hehe, someone giggled. Rallied and titillated.

"Old age is the same for everybody," the senior shepherd stated. "The first water makes you wet."

He kept glancing around. He ended up staring at a spot in the corner, the first to absorb the evening darkness, where the chair, in bad condition, was spilling out its straw. They all stared at it. But then the boy got down on his knees and begged them to play one of their carols. So they stood up and gladly put on their instruments again.

The kid stayed on his knees on the step at the base of the fireplace. Stooped over, he was moving his hands and rolling his fingers to the rhythm of those sweet and stringy sounds the way you roll dough. He smiled at the men, turning here and there, with bright eyes and the light reflecting off his forehead. They watched him as they listened, absorbed, and filled with tenderness.

A sweet and sour voice, primordial, like the bleat of the lamb. An ancestral voice. So pathetically evocative. A voice that smells like oranges and fresh manure. That sounds like festivals, innocent joy, and happy childish excitement. With the flavor of yesterday. Under the blur of their childhood memories, the men totter toward the shepherds standing in the middle of the kitchen. Heavens! What a peaceful Christmas sound. The time we were all brothers, ah . . . the pipers, the people from the same mountain who now might be enemies.

Old Baboro was agitated, too, coming up out of a feverish sleepiness where maybe he had been holding little Baborino's hand, walking on the frozen snow of the path toward the church, through the night's pealing bells. But with a gurgle of cough in his chest, he woke up completely, only to find himself in the room. And he made a strange gesture, maybe to his companions or maybe to the instruments, a gesture of rejection and recrimination. I believe he had spotted the rubber. Instead of real animal skins, the bagpipers used a piece of inner tube that swelled like a leech; even bagpipes were a sham.

He got up, dragging his feet, and Alleluia followed him to put him to bed. The young shepherd said, "That one already has gotten wet."

2. It was a night of anxiety and fear. The two men insisted on staying by the fireplace, stretched out on the benches with their haversacks under their heads. The others kept inviting them to make themselves comfortable on folding beds in one of the cells, but the older shepherd, leaning on his elbows, replied by rote, "Some make their nest in the burrow, others on the branch." And after delivering that verdict, he lay back down and shut his mouth decisively. In the end they had to leave them alone and the door was closed. Through the door cracks, they could see the older one twice get up and snoop around. Franzè was on guard duty, but nobody else was thinking yet of tucking in for the night.

The woman was taken by a whim to go out. Outside, in the open air. Vanzi went to her cell, voices leaked out from under her door. The seminarian too had left his cell. Without some fresh air, stuck there, the woman must have felt her head would burst: the seminarian offered to go with her. Alright then. Franzè, by the low wall, would keep an eye on her, and at the first suspicious move drive a bullet into her body. They had already gone back to being cruel.

They had to give in to her request. Followed by the priest, La Rossa, all wrapped up in her cloak, made her way between the men. Everybody had taken up a weapon, fearing — those two in the kitchen, the woman outside, the thick woods all around — an ambush. Peeping through the cracks, Divinangelo signaled that the old shepherd had raised his head up. What if they were partisans in disguise? A hand on his holster, Vanzi was limping back and forth on his rubber soles. He stopped at the door with everybody, barefoot, behind him. In the pale churchyard, the two figures were walking slowly. In the center rose the high dark cross; in the background, upright, they could see Franzè's rifle. The white moonlight filtered through to them and Vanzi's forehead seemed as white as paper. Alleluia's earrings shone. Someone blew out the fading lamp.

And only when they saw him leaving the kitchen did they remember the boy. Annaloro promptly grabbed him by the ears, but he was laughing. "'Hey Pops,' I said to him, 'what is keeping you from sleeping if your bagpipes are here, safe?'" He was laughing, cracking himself up between tears and snot. "He is looking for the little chair, he claims his little chair has been stolen."

He is Panipuccio the shepherd — someone whispered — right, he is the same Panipuccio who made the little chair with his own hands as an offering to the monastery, maybe as a vow.

"He says it's joined, crafted without glue or nails, and it was stolen, that's what he says."

Freeing himself, the boy ran to the empty cell of the prisoner to retrieve the little chair with the back, carrying it into the kitchen over his head, like a trophy, to calm down the strange old man.

3. I find some notes about another time she went out late — based on the phase of the moon, it must have been earlier. She usually was given a period to exercise in the morning, but this time she demanded to go out again. She insisted. The seminarian, as always,

interceded to have her request granted. The churchyard was lit by the last daylight and the first outline of the moon.

"It looks like a blade," the woman said, pointing at the razor-sharp sickle in the sky.

He replied, "It looks like an opening."

She admitted he was right: it looked like a small crack, too. She pulled back the hood of her cloak from her forehead and opened her mouth to quench her thirst for fresh air, like she always used to do once she was outdoors.

"You really," the young man hastily murmured, "do not believe in God?"

She laughed. "What a question."

"Do you believe in Him?"

She threw a glance at him. "This is not a question to be asked point-blank."

"Do you believe in Him?" he insisted, lowering his head.

"Listen to him. After pressing me to talk for so long . . . he starts again from the beginning."

She moved. He followed her. "You have to answer me, now."

"And why not?" she decided, wrapping herself in the cloak. "Here, I don't know for sure. Or, maybe better, I know that we must not believe in Him anymore."

It was not the answer; on the contrary, it was a provocation he would have to blunt. But the woman walked firmly ahead, refusing the confrontation.

He brought up the subject again back in her cell, and more than once. Confidently, almost carelessly, she would come out with something like: we have to free ourselves of God. And calmly explained her thinking affirming that by now He Himself rejects us. Just like a mother who moves the child away from her skirt so that he can learn to walk alone.

"They say it?" the priest insinuated.

"They who? You are smart, kid. But I don't want to give you an answer. . . . Besides, I have thought and thought about it until I burst my brains. I'm the one who says these things and that's that."

She was laughing, covering her mouth with her hand, like shy peasant women do. Her ideas were written in the notebook. A notebook, she said, full of errors. She had no intention of showing it to him; he was the type who would grab the red and blue pencils to mark it up—like our schoolteacher who's right here with us.

"But maybe, in the end, I will have to leave it in your hands," she added.

She would come up with absurdities like this, capable of annihilating a priest. God, again, "since he had been trotted out." It seemed to her that men never serve the Creator's will more than when they are making war. War has been given to them, like wings to birds, so that they can rise up. "War is the mother of all things." Blushing, she quoted Herodotus—without mentioning his name.

"That has been said already, as I recall. Before Christ."

"Ah! And so? I can see by myself that even the most civilized man immediately adapts to war as if it were his second nature. Look at how excited the boy is. A doubled vitality. And the others, these despicable little peasants and petty bourgeois, see how they threw themselves into the fray. Even our unarmed schoolteacher—not suited for war."

"They believed in it."

"Right. Everybody thinks his own war is good. So long as he thinks he can win. Wait, wait and see when this one will be over. Soon they'll all again begin to say that they are working for peace. Because, look, whoever wants to improve his status wants war. Whoever defends his status also wants it. But above of all, whoever intends to reform the world wants it. And maybe we want it more than anyone else."

The young man talked little, but he was not intimidated. He could sometimes even astonish her. Smiling, annoying her with that "Do they say so?," he suggested that they were wrong to speak in such terms because men do not want to live without . . ."without believing in something."

"Well, they'd better wean themselves, they'd better wean themselves of that."

Every once in a while she would exclaim, "He understood me, oh! He is a peasant, he is. I have always enjoyed talking to peasants. They are never surprised or scandalized."

"The peasant is never scandalized. But try to separate him from his beliefs. He is a rock."

"And we too are peasants—we're rocks. Even so, time is like water, it brings everything back to dust. But now we are hearing about a new weapon that can sweep everything away before you can say 'Amen.' Whoever gets it first, will win this war. And maybe after the war it will be necessary to sterilize an infected world again, and start from the beginning."

He countered that starting all over again would be a waste of time.

"Hey, you, peasant, every season nature starts again from the beginning, cool days don't turn right into warm days."

"On the contrary, it's just like that. What is dead decays into soil and produces new humus."

Certain answers thrilled her. She promised herself she would write them down. Decaying in order to be revived. The dead leaf must fall, so that it will rot and sprout.

"Did you finally get it? This is how we want to start again, just like nature."

"But the dry leaf must fall by itself. Besides, nature is God. You do not have the power . . . you human beings."

"We do. You prune and throw the pieces in the fire, no? Ash fertilizes too. Everything has the power to follow nature's laws so why shouldn't men? On the contrary, it's time that they renounce imposture once and for all. Without you. Leave us alone."

"You and your people have already tried that, didn't you?"

"Alright. You're an astute priest. As soon as any of you wear the cassock you turn into snakes and the dove flies away. But tell me, have you ever wondered how these ideas could come out of my head if my mind is stuck in ignorance? I have chiseled them. I have done it with my own hands. But there are people who use a hammer and chisel on the great collective head, to open it once and for all."

She stood up, raising her arms, as if she were issuing a threat.

"You people smash heads," he said. "I knew it." A harsh, conclusive tone. With that same tone he added, "You have smashed Baborino's head." And left the cell, striding out in the open air.

He had spoken to her with authority. It was as if he had hit her full-on with that rash accusation. At the time I couldn't explain it.

4. When they came back to the kitchen, next to the fire, they both looked thinner; the woman's breasts hung down to her belly. The priest, bent over, placed his gnarled hands on his bony knees, leaning on himself for support. As if talking wastes away the talkers. Those obscure exchanges that had intrigued the men whenever they could overhear the most heated remarks. And the priest now knows everything. (But he didn't know anything yet.) Their tongues had suddenly dried up, they were just staring, the two of them, with a sort of arcane bewilderment. The men, too, were feeling enervated, and their sad, bristly beards sprouted on their pallid cheeks. The woman pushed out her legs, swishing her cloak, revealing ribbed stockings made of raw wool. Like their wives, she wore simple clothes and didn't wash herself very often. A woman's odor by a hearth is always perturbing to men.

Somebody said, "In the village people are getting ready for the festivities."

The night before they had discussed whether they could go down for a short visit before Christmas.

"Our folks don't know that we are still here," Baboro observed. "If the pipers have talked, they might believe we've already left."

His voice was wheezy, the way wind sounds in a broken whistle, but he had no fever. (God, as the saying goes, does not make the shorn sheep feel the cold.) "Heaven help us," he added, "we would be in trouble if they knew." He was referring to the women. Silence fell again.

Those two, the priest and La Rossa, were no longer like the others. The fragile balance reestablished during their absence was again broken. Quiet hours spent by the fireplace like those they used to have at home. (In the mountains people know how to stare endlessly, without getting bored, at the flame's language and the patterns of the swirling snow.) And then, the Germans. And then, the pipers. In spite of everything, those had been distractions. They don't get along well with her, her and the priest. It's troubling to look at the gaunt faces of those two. The night of the pipers she tempted fate, she probably thought, too, of an ambush, that they had come to rescue her, she was ready in the churchyard with the defenseless young man. And if they had taken her back, well, if they really had taken her back . . . but here she is again, enormous, looming.

The circle expanded, they were all there. And it started all over again. And she was the one to blame. She did it in a way that seemed spontaneous. (But it was eventually clear that she had figured it out. Ha, she wanted to demolish the priest.) The little boy was making a pair of shoes from two large slices of pigskin for anyone whose soles had worn out. With a curved rasp in his hand, frowning and sticking out his tongue, he was using all his strength to cut around an outline he had traced as the shoemaker Divinangelo looked on. The seminarian was watching him, laughing; in fact, he burst out laughing with his mouth wide open, like a child himself.

The woman stares at his mouth, stares at him for a while, then says, "Your teeth are like sugared almonds; they seem made to be licked."

They all laughed, even Vanzi laughed, his bald head blushing. "Ha-ha," Divinangelo shrieked, "have you made love in there or what?" Alleluia loudly pounded his thighs, bursting into his wolfish laugh. And Franzè: "Don't be offended, men like to joke."

66

She gave a little contrite laugh. "I didn't mean to be offensive. As for mine, well, you can see for yourselves. He has white nicely rooted teeth and fresh gums. People from the countryside have great teeth. Anyone would want to look them in the mouth — look at Baboro, there he is, laughing, his teeth are black, but he still has all of them. We common city folk, we lose them early. The young man here, he's the son of a yokel, he's solid. So what's wrong with that? Can't I say that I like his mouth?"

She took her hair out of her gap-toothed comb, and held it up. "I will never have a child like him, this one has already suffered in his mother's womb. And when I was a child I used to eat boiled potatoes, no calcium, I was not like a chicken that could pick some up as I roamed around on the ground. Hey you, you who has it in for whores, how much do you think someone like me could make, with my teeth, bad since I was a girl?"

(But they did think that she had made a lot, seeing her so plump, delicious as any fat woman — the kind who is much appreciated in the countryside.)

All at once, she put the comb back into her mane, leaving out half of that thick tangle. "There he is, the little grass snake with his mouth open and his twisted little teeth. You, if you have bad teeth, it's because you've been given too much sugar to eat."

Offended, the kid retorted, "They're not bad at all," and went back sullenly to cutting.

"Well, anyway, when you are forty you'll have a nice gold-dotted rack. These touchy, petty bourgeoisie don't let themselves be spoiled without defending themselves. But him, our dear priest, he will keep them like sugared almonds."

They fell to commenting: she has it in for him, eh? Malicious giggles. They took a naive pleasure, a little devious, thinking she had it in for the priest.

"But what are you saying, fools? For him? He's such an honest, respectable boy. Maybe, if he eventually dedicates himself to the pleasures of the table . . . . Priests, at a certain point, become keen on good food, food is from God too."

"They just nibble on a hen boiled in water," Divinangelo shrieked. "What on earth is a hen boiled in water?"

"They just want to pull your leg," Franzè said.

Vanzi was sitting on the bench, not at all at ease, forcing himself to smile at the corners of his mouth. "Right," he commented, "men joke, they need to joke."

And the boy, daring, "He is like a toad who's been pelted with stones."

Baboro gravely uttered, "Eh, my little priest, they are backbiters, that's what they are."

Alleluia touched the cassock with his pointing finger and passed one of his judgments: "He who squats too low gets smeared with shit."

The others openly laughed at the homespun saying. Without parting his lips, the young man smiled too and looked at the apprentice whose laugh sounded like a whinny.

And suddenly the unpleasant feeling arose that they had started to quarrel again, just to kill time. But what a woman, what an impudent woman. And then, since everybody was there, the plan to go renew the supplies for Christmas was debated once more. It had stopped snowing. But was it necessary, after the somewhat suspicious visit by the pipers, to go? And with the Germans up there? They were convinced that no, it was better to wait it out. The boy said that he had no intention to go back to the village ever again. He dangled a piece of pigskin as if he were shaking the dust off a pair of shoes. And Divinangelo tugged at his short mangy beard and laid it on thicker: damn village. They were all feeling bold.

And sitting there, quietly, there she was, with her warm, savory face, fat and full-breasted like a domestic pigeon.

5. Alleluia and the boy went to find the tree. They climbed down the hard ground of the slope in their uncomfortable shoes until they

found the right Christmas tree, a little fir. Caressing the thin needles with their fingertips, they invited me to admire it. The rough swineherd, too.

Worried about the little one, I had followed them—my boots were still holding up. When Alleluia would pass through the villages hoisting his pig gelder's stick, the pigs, closed in their pens, would start screaming like terrified Christians. There were stories about his awful assaults on animals, even sex; they said he could satisfy a donkey in heat. And apparently he had maimed and then killed one by thrusting and stirring a stick inside. Maybe those were just boasts and lies, but even when he was going to the stable to look after our animals, if the boy followed him, I would keep an eye on them. If the mule was unruly as he dragged him out, he would give it a sound thrashing. The woman's donkey had escaped and couldn't be found.

They started digging on their hands and knees around the tree. Finally, the last rosy roots pulled free. Alleluia left his hands amid the soil and roots, stirring them with a sort of voluptuous pleasure. On the way back, carrying the tree on his shoulders, his big face, fresh and wild, ruddy amid the green needles, looked like a pig's head roasting in rosemary.

The fir tree received a merry welcome. Someone would always be busy circling around it, hanging this or that from the boughs. Even Baboro hung up one of the charms from his silver pocket watch. Using the tinfoil from Hans's chocolates, they made ornaments and fringes and a Bethlehem star with a swishing long tail to pin at the top. The boy stuck on the CHORUS frame as well, its slightly darkened gold and arcane letters seemed to project a halo of mystical glory. Vanzi sacrificed one of our candles to make a set of tiny ones. The seminarian made wicks from the bits of thread he picked up in the woman's cell.

But suddenly she started laughing at them as they had all gathered around, dawdling. Oh sure, Christmas. They hang up some glittering gewgaws on a poor plant and say it's Christmas. And then, that night, they'll pass the time growing sad around the fire because they miss the smell of anchovies and the beds they share with their wives. Christmas without a Christmas Eve dinner and without a woman. Ha-ha. They won't be able to stand such deprivations, they won't, poor people.

The men did not breathe a word. Openly disappointed, they thought, she has it in for everyone, this woman. Disappointed and embittered. Like children riding a broom who feel the steed between their legs and then someone starts reminding them, out of spite, that it's just a broom, just a wooden stick. It was not a Christmas tree, indeed, it was not going to be Christmas, and they knew it. But they hated the woman for saying it out loud. At night, next to the fire, they loved staring in the semidarkness into the corner, the vague, starred splendor radiating from the silver dangling on the fringed branches and the glorious halo of the CHORUS sign. And in spite of it all, she did not become less harsh; they were bewildered. Teasing the priest was one thing, quite common, after all. Talking nonsense and bragging were still alright, they didn't use proper language either, and they cursed—God always forgives His own—like sailors. But a sacred tree, the reverence, the yearning, the pang that some things continue to instill . . . ah, some things are untouchable. It is true that that woman has no religion. She doesn't believe in God. In that realization was something dreadful, a sense of something irrevocable between them that was as well an incurable hostility. And in some way, it provided them with an excuse.

That time they all looked at me. You, teacher, you never take a stand. It was as if they were coming out and saying it to me. That I belonged with those in the Book of Revelations, neither hot nor cold—lukewarm.

6. The night before Christmas Eve, nobody was talking. They were all as mute and stiff as logs—a large, scattered circle—all waiting for her to leave. Her presence made them bitter to the core. Pa-

70

thetically, with a deep resentment, they felt they were victims. They were the victims. Her prisoners.

She realized that and decided to start a quarrel.

"You," flaring up to the seminarian, "you believe that by allowing men to light a few small candles on Christmas Eve you can still snare them?" She pointed at the decorated tree. "Eh, you actually believe it's going to go on like that? I mean, after this war. Look at their faces, c'mon. While they are waiting to kill, they think this ridiculous homage will please God. Or maybe they do it for themselves, to fool themselves and to pass the time. But the party's already spoiled, look at them."

The boy had fallen asleep on the bench. He was sleeping soundly, his head over Divinangelo's pointy knees. He didn't wake up.

"And there will not be any party for a long time," the woman was raising her voice more and more. "Neither celebrations nor peace. Afterward, you know that, eh? It's going to be worse. Hell has opened and all the devils are loose."

Alleluia said, "Now she plays the astrologer." He winced and flashed his wolfish teeth at her, his brutish sneer.

And Franzè, to the priest contentiously: "Just like a toad under the stones. Answer her, go on, answer her."

"Just make her shut up once and for all," Divinangelo mumbled. And he tenderly stretched his hand over the sleeping child.

"Ha-ha, they are afraid to listen to me, that's how they are. But I want to paint the whole picture. I like getting you riled up." The woman was casting her flaming gaze around the intimidated silence. "This is nothing. When this is over, and God only knows how, there will still be war and it will last forever. The chain of reprisals will never stop. But for all of these ones here, no need to go very far. Their bill will be paid sooner rather than later. Your God takes his reprisals, too. He who says, 'Vengeance is mine.'"

She was pointing an accusing finger, and she petrified them. And then she turned her finger to the priest, with a more and more menacing voice. "Maybe men will be hung again by their feet and their genitals, eh? You have given us an old and illustrious example in the slaughter of the Vandeans. But maybe something better has been imagined and we don't know it yet. Who knows? For example, a radical genocide. Men are headed in that direction — they no longer make a distinction between a splash of blood and a mass slaughter."

The child's wailing interrupted her. He was crying in his sleep. That unconscious voice, which pierced the men in their guts, seemed to spur her on.

"And then the peace will come. Ah, what a peace. It's not easy to shake off the ferocity of war. Sure, people will return to the ways they've always lived, adjusting the armchair as they read the newspaper, taking a nap after lunch. There will be newspapers again, sure. And simply following the crime news will be enough: you'll see there will be everything, every sort of thing. And the children will still be the ones who pay. Not even counting those riddled with bullets who will remain scattered on the earth. Besides, every house will have plenty of munitions; people have grown used to weapons. New Year's Eves will be celebrated with the shots of battles; at midnight people will die just as they do in a war. All sorts of things will appear in the newspapers during peacetime. And if this horrible peace that awaits us helps people understand enough is enough, that peace will be good, for it's been useful. Maybe someone eventually will win, really, once and for all. In fact, I already know who will win. What do you think, priest? You got me. And don't put on that pitying expression. Don't treat me like a madwoman, I forbid you to."

"No, no," he said in a soothing tone of voice. "And there will be weeping and gnashing of teeth. This has been written as well. But you . . . your head is a museum of horrors, you . . . ." And with that truncated phrase he was staring at her.

"The museum of horrors is inside each of us," she shouted, in a renewed paroxysm. "That's already been discovered." And sagging, looking exhausted and distraught, she added, "Hell is on earth."

"Amen," Baboro unexpectedly replied, and made the sign of the cross.

"We will light the candles," said the seminarian, looking around firmly and reassuringly. "It may well be that these men will kill with their same hands. But you . . . ."

The woman vehemently spat into the fire and started laughing. Her long laughter came in bursts, shaking her belly. Jolted, she was holding her body with her hands. And maybe that was a labor pain. For the umpteenth time she terrorized them. They were ready for that step; they couldn't wait to get out of it. But now that the labor was late, it would be a really nasty way to spoil their celebration — and she's capable of it. No doubt she would have tormented them up to her last breath about the tree and the poor little candles.

It was the seminarian who took up a glass of water and sprinkled her as if he were performing an exorcism. Then he escorted her back to the cell.

In the sudden silence the kid had woken up. He smiled at everyone.

VII

1. The boy was the first to hear the approaching, thudding, rhythm of hooves and breaking branches. Darting out, he saw the mule and the women. He raised the alarm with his little wolf cub's call — *uhuu*. At the end of the churchyard, Alleluia lifted his rifle high and shot a booming blank shot. The windows and doors slammed and a sound arose of pattering feet and excited voices.

Everyone gathered around the women and the fully loaded mule. Franzè's Menina and Annaloro's Madelona had arrived. Franzè rushed out in his undershirt, a patch of hair sprouting from his chest and his stony cheeks turning red. Mad, mad women. He was trying to grab his Menina by the waist. She dodged him, laughing, and gave him a nudge in the ribs. Annaloro, wearing a concentrated and tense expression, circled silently around his Madelona as if he were performing a figure from a country dance. Shaking the rifle, Alleluia and the boy jumped all around between clucks and shouts, for the boy was hugging a little hen.

It was a moment of loud cheerfulness, as if they found themselves in the plot of a western — that is, in a fiction.

"Christ!" Franzè suddenly burst out, "What if you had met the patrol?"

Menina opened her large mouth with its big white teeth. "We

came here with the night patrol halfway up the side of the mountain." She seemed not to care about the sudden silence. She had
seen the priest and went to bow to him. Madelona did the same.

Their hobnail steps joyfully echoed through the kitchen. Leaving
all the work to the women, the men sat down in comfort, lighting
their pipes, and watched them bustling about. The prisoner left her
cell at the usual time and calmly went to take her usual spot on the
bench. In the turmoil, a few of the men had warned her not to move,
but forgot to lock her in. Loudly going on with the housework, the
women didn't even turn their eyes in her direction. Madelona was
right under the stranger's nose, her big bottom draped by the wide
creased pleats of her skirt as she bent over to stir the minced barley
in the coffeepot over the fire. Watching how Menina started tapping
her heels, her husband realized she already knew. His flabby lips lost
their grip around the stem of his pipe. His self-confidence failed at
the same time. They were all contrite now, spying on the women
with elusive glances.

La Rossa sniffed. "Oh oh, you got anchovies." And added, dripping with sarcasm, "And wives."

The boy had grabbed the hen, holding it firmly in his arms. He let
the seminarian lead him out of the room. In the hallway, they ran
into Vanzi.

"Mister Don Silvino, good morning," Menina recited in a formal
tone of voice. Madelona echoed her.

"Good morning, good morning." Vanzi frowned. "I don't know
if . . . I mean . . . did they . . . have you been introduced . . . ?"

They thumped their hobnailed boots. Madelona, turning her brawny
back, stopped by the stove while the slim Menina kept rapidly bustling about, snapping her skirt.

"Come, come and have a seat, Mister Don Silvino," La Rossa teased.

And completely absorbed in his thoughts, he walked across the room
like a robot. His hands trembled while he nervously lit a cigarette.

"No need," Menina said in a shrill voice as she turned to her husband. "No need to introduce me. Ah, this is a good one. What?" (Franzè had not said a word.) "I, I know everything, we know very well." She poured a heap of flour on the table, raising a puff, and made a well in the center rapidly with her fist. "Everyone knows."

"What . . . what, what do they know?" Vanzi asked.

"It's because you don't even think of listening to women and so you end up in the worst troubles." Holding an egg, she was stretching out her arm, keeping her husband at bay. "You wanted to go? And now you're paying the piper." She broke the egg on the table with a harsh knock that gave Franzè a start. "Everybody, everybody knows about it."

"Tell me, woman," Baboro intervened, "what are you chatting about? What does everybody know?"

Shaking her hips, Menina loudly broke more eggs and started beating them into the flour with closed fingers. "That you are stuck, for example. That you have . . ." She whirled her finger forcefully, raising more puffs of flour. "You wait for her to deliver, eh?"

"C'mon, speak up," Vanzi ordered her. "Who knows about it?"

"Everybody knows. Half of the village knows. And those who took to the woods know as well. Even the devil knows about it. Eh, Madelona?" she called her compatriot as witness. Without turning, Madelona shook her hips. "Eh, Menina?" "You go ahead." Annaloro nodded to his wife and she silently bent her head over the anchovy sauce that was sending out an intense aroma.

"They took the Falone men. Yes, the Germans. Yes, they took the old man as well." Menina kept kneading, furiously thrusting her fingers in the dough, addressing nobody. "Just like that. And at the Rapina a shack exploded. Two Germans were wounded. They have shot Riccione and Nico di Bongioco, the men from the sheepfolds."

Divinangelo said, "They had taken to the woods."

"Right, to the Incoronata caves."

"Eh, what did I say?" Divinangelo triumphantly claimed.

"You said it, eh? Yeah, you are so good. You said it? Well, by now they are not there anymore. Now the Germans are at the Rapina and the ones who were hiding in the caves are not there anymore. And now you are here."

Alleluia jubilantly shouted, "Then I will not take a turn at surveillance anymore, there's no point in it."

"There's no point in it," Menina repeated, her voice growing more shrill. "There's absolutely no point in it. Who would come to get her? Forgive me Don Silvino, but I do have to say this. A pregnant woman does not tempt anybody." She slapped the piece of dough on the table with such force that the men were startled.

"The Germans don't know about it," Vanzi hazarded.

"They don't know, eh? They don't know anything unless you inform them?—them, the Germans? They leave her to you, they're happy to leave her to you, they aren't eager to take on this trouble. They leave her to you. You have to be the one to take care of it, to straighten out the neck for the hatchet . . . . They leave you alone as long as you want, you're the boss here, they're even grateful to you. You put your hands on her first, that was some great stroke of luck."

"Yeah, well, I caught her," Franzè could not stay quiet.

"You did?" She slapped the dough over and over. "You're so good. You found a treasure, you big brute. And don't worry, nobody will snatch it away. You have to keep her with you. Your teeth will have to chatter while she delivers the child. And what you go through while we deliver is nothing. Your teeth will keep chattering until the moment you can drag her out and fire your gun at her. No, you aren't even allowed to give it all a second thought, they won't let you. And you have to carry the burden of that in your soul throughout this life and the next, and it will eventually weigh down your children, too . . . weigh on those innocent . . . ."

Bursting into tears, hiding her face behind her apron, she ran out, leaving Madelona to take over the kneading and the men struck dumb.

2. The Germans didn't look surprised to find the kitchen full of women, at least two of whom were very big. Even Hans's quiet fellow soldier noticed the bench by the fireplace, covered by the women's wide skirts. They were speaking in dialect, but he seemed to be eavesdropping anyway.

("Is it moving?" "Yes, it's alive." "It starts to be heavy, eh?" "By the end the weight hangs like a plumb and the belly lowers." "Do you feel it lower?" "It's getting lower, yes, it's heavy.")

Hans was carrying presents for the boy, rich chunks of chocolate, a sort of dense cake, and two little greenish oranges from the coast, which spread their evocative perfume all through the kitchen. Nobody was enthusiastic about the idea of lighting — by daylight and in front of that pair of Germans — the little candles on the tree; it almost seemed like a sacrilege. But the boy insisted. He and Hans got to work with the matches. The young German had left his weapon in a corner. When he threw away his half-smoked cigarette, I could picture him in the storeroom of the house that would burn, letting a cigarette butt drop so he could pet his beloved little white horse.

When the shutters were closed and all the candles had been lit — not one was missed — and the solemn gold-framed CHORUS seemed so magnificent as it hung there, no one could doubt that it was an authentic Christmas tree. In the shadowed room, the downy treetop turned silver, radiating moonlight. Enraptured, solemn, they drew as one closer to the tree. Hans bowed, gathering the light on his golden curls, and almost scorching his hair. His fellow soldier, too, half-kneeling, finally decided to lay down the machine gun. Both were trustful and disarmed. Only the women, sprawled on the bench, providing cover for each other, had not moved. But no one was looking at them anymore.

The boy reverently lifted the CHORUS sign and handed it to his friend Hans, who knew Latin. The German pronounced the word three times in a row — an arcane spelling — and three times he bowed his thanks. The two left soon after. We never knew what they had talked about with Vanzi. Besides, letting them see three women to-gether, deceptively, had been a good thing.

La Rossa demanded both of the little greenish oranges, which were as hard as pebbles. Her craving contracted her face. A pregnant woman with a craving could have a miscarriage. She didn't even leave a peel for the kid, she bit into them and avidly sucked their sour flavor. She spent the whole afternoon there next to the fire without a word and then finally left. She asked to be locked in.

Once she was out of the picture, it was almost a real Christmas Eve. The table in the refectory was long and crowded, carefully laid out, with plenty of candles and wine and sweets, even if the bowls didn't match. The faded saints swayed from the frescoes in elusive benevolence. The tree had been carried closer and the candles were lit again. And once more they were enraptured and moved. At the boy's feet, the hen was pecking the crumbs on the ground, gur-gling in her domestic way and fluttering onto the table every now and then.

The two couples stayed close. Annaloro suddenly would brush his hand over Madelona's wide skirts, as if he wanted to be sure of her solid presence. Franzè, his narrow eyes wide open to look at his Menina, flashed a tender gray light from under his dark lashes. He was holding her secretly, too—by the waist, while she was chatting in her lively way with everybody, giving updates on all the local news, private as well as public. She had started off with me by saying "Zaira sends her best," making me blush. I thought that my affair with the young woman was still a secret.

"And your kids," she says to Vanzi, who in fact didn't ask, "are doing well. And your Missus Anna always prays." "Thank you, Menina." "And your little Miss Lisa has done her hair up into a braided crown like a lady." "Really, Menina?" "And the little Mister Nico has put the Nativity figures on the moss and says that they're making war. And the plaster goats are the Englishmen." "Really, Menina?" "Really. They can't think about anything else. Like all of you. Fanatical about the war." "Certainly not, Menina." "Then why did you leave? Your children always talk about you and you aren't there."

Franzè says, "What are you thinking, Menina? And who would stop by for a shave, the dogs? Nobody was coming anymore. And the shop?" "They broke your windows and the mirror with stones." "You see?" "You have been a bully," replies Menina, sadly, caressing his hard curls. He has soaked his hair so much with water, trying to tame his curls, that they are stuck to his skull. "I didn't want to shave the Germans, that's all."

Englishmen and *Germans*, they pronounced the words like D'Annunzio did, but that tickled the boy's sense of humor. He was snuffing the candles, delicately, with his sensitive little fingers. They all stared at him, remembering the Nativity scene at his house, the old Bellorio house that had burnt down. A large Nativity scene in the hall, assembled by the old man over many weeks; the whole village would file in to admire it. Only maybe the kid didn't remember it, for he was totally absorbed by that prodigious sparkling tree he had created with his own hands. He demanded the tree be brought back into the kitchen so he could still enjoy it. Make him stop, make him stop bothering everybody. But four men lifted and carried it again and made sure it didn't lose even the tiniest lump of wax.

Before midnight the women wanted to go to church. Pressing against their husbands' sides, they were dead tired, but their request, too, was granted. First were the two couples, next Divinangelo taking the docile boy by the hand, and Baboro with Alleluia, all going ahead in pairs for the procession; last, at a distance, Vanzi and I. Four towering lamps whose flickering halo looked like a wavering host. The light touched here and there a miter, the fragmented robes of priests and angels, trumpets' mouthpieces, two pale feet, and the necrotic cheek of a bishop.

The seminarian was there waiting, kneeling on the stairs, just as if the altar were still there. He evidently had swept and cleaned up as if it really were a church. But then, at that moment, it was a real church for the men as well. Menina pulled down Franzè to kneel next to her, Annaloro kneeled with his Madelona. And the women were gazing with such passion at their men, grown wild behind those beards. All around, the others. And they all kissed the tiny sacred corpse on the ice-cold palm of the seminarian, brass on a black cross. Born and crucified.

3. All of a sudden, the sky silently collapsed to the earth. Since morning it had been low and white, almost grazing the woods. It was turning dark. Large, dense, heavy flakes fell like a screen. The whole world sinks. Christ was born in vain. They thought about their women, at home by now, about their home fires. A deep despair weighed on the men. Not a glimmer of the Christmas consolation. None of the high spirits of the morning after. Nervous, excessive spirits. And, on second thought, inappropriate ones. That was when the two husbands, leaving the cells where they had slept with their wives, had shown up in the kitchen vamping in the women's crocheted-lace underwear. The others had danced around them, as in a masquerade, overexcited and shouting. The days before the festivity, those same two, Franzè and Annaloro, claiming they knew how, had done the laundry and ended up reducing their underwear to black rags. Without using a cloth as a filter, they had poured ashes and boiling water at the same time over their underwear and shirts. For days they had been walking around with their legs held wide, their private parts chafed from the rough contact with their pants. Now they felt uncomfortable with the fresh linen down there, the tight crotches and tickling laces.

It was as dark as if night were falling. Divinangelo, looking more gaunt than usual, drew a lit twig close to the lamp's spout. Under the flickering light, they saw each other's resentful faces, the shameful faces of sinners. The seminarian, his head bowed, opened his breviary and plunged into reading. The prisoner kept her eyes closed, her belly rising up with every breath like a wineskin. They felt ashamed for keeping her there, in that condition, waiting to kill her. That was the moment when no one felt capable anymore of doing it.

In the far, dark corner, the boy, with the hen on his shoulder, was bustling around his tree. The candles had smeared and scorched the feathery needles. Pulling and tearing, he was stripping the tree down completely, relentlessly demolishing it. A murdered tree. And his witchy hen with her fixed, vitreous eye and her manure dropping all over everything: it was time to twist her neck.

"Hey you, there," Franzè shouted, "you can eat those branches at this point."

The boy replied: "Drop dead." The hen flapped to keep her balance. Completely tamed, she was hanging onto his shoulder as if it were a beam in the hen house.

They lit their pipes again; they were packed with the dried herbs the women had brought for the herbal teas. The women had brought sugar and coffee as well, two small packets, and ordered the men to keep them for the mother-to-be. Women can always find everything. Men, though, waste things. There already was no more tobacco.

Closing her eyes, La Rossa turned up her nose at that herbal smoke and, her stomach reeling, proclaimed, "Skunks!"

"You smell like piss," Alleluia retorted. But the others did not talk.

"You skunks," she attacked. "You smell like billy goats after your blessed night." She opened her gloomy eyes. "Did you have your Christmas? Did you have your taste of anchovies and women? You stuffed yourselves and let loose, eh? And now you've got heartburn."

Those two couples in the cells, the emanations of their lovemaking warming up the icy-cold hallway, excited the lonely ones in their hard beds, maybe even the miserable Divinangelo, who was jealous of the hen, and Alleluia, who left his cell naked, jerking his thing like an aspergillum: harsh, she seemed to hold everything against them, even the things she had not seen. Her angry diatribe went on and on, she mocked the men ferociously, and they took it without a word.

At a certain point they went back to their pipes, puffing out the smoke of linden, chamomile, and mallow, slowly relaxing. Everything was as usual. She insults them, backbiting. Everything was back to normal. Who knows how long it would go on.

4. But it started exactly like it usually did at home — they were caught unawares.

Since morning, taking turns, the men went out for short walks in the snow, trading off the same pair of tall rubber boots to protect their worn-out shoes. The snow was high but still soft; they could sink up to their knees. A cold, dazzling sun, and clouds running up through the spreading blue of the sky. All around, diamond rays spurted from each rounded surface and from the snow-covered boughs. The boy took out his little hen, too, and she swerved with each step, blinded by the whiteness.

Her head dangling, waking up with a sudden start, the woman dozed for hours. Two or three times already Annaloro had whispered, "The baby is bouncing," but no one paid attention to him. They were all nodding around the fireplace. The seminarian at some point asked her, "What is wrong?" Raising her breasts off her belly, she mumbled that she had had some labor pains since the morning.

It seemed as if no one had heard her. Then suddenly Annaloro, as an expert in laundry and delivery, jumped up and went to rinse the cauldron. He filled it, then hung it by a chain over the flame, checking again for the clarity of the water inside. The men depended again on his oracular powers, for he was an experienced husband who knew all about women's things. The boy was ordered to feed the fire in the woman's cell. He took the hen with him, his inseparable Conchita that seemed glued to his shoulder. Divinangelo followed. Everyone stood up. Alleluia walked around the kitchen twice, then, like an executioner, grabbed the axe and ran outside as if he intended to cut down the snow-covered trees.

"The linen," Baboro asked, agitated, "the linen, where do you keep it?"

The woman was silently writhing in pain as her labor grew in force. Panting, she warned, "Stop swarming around like bumblebees. I know what to do." She tightened her lips at the crash as Franzè dumped the pile of logs right next to her.

"We need a strong fire," Annaloro pressed. "It must boil. We need boiling water. When my wife is giving birth, I am always given the job of boiling water."

"Just to get you out of their way," La Rossa teased, recovering in a moment of temporary relief. "Are you afraid I might get an infection in the next world?" She lay down on her back, relaxing her numb body.

"Is it better?" the seminarian asked.

She replied sharply, "Soon it will get worse."

5. When she retired to her cell, they all went along, looking like a funeral escort. Vanzi was there too. In his dispassionate tone, he acknowledged that it had started. Through the door's cracks, the big fire the boy had fed sent out a ruddy glimmer. The laboring woman went in and, following her orders, the door was locked from the outside. The door could be reopened only by her order. The men immediately started tiptoeing and whispering, as if they were at the house of someone gravely ill. They asked the boy to eavesdrop; they were almost frightened, and at first they did not dare to do it. But nothing could be heard except the crackling of the resinous fire. A smell, too, could be sensed, vaguely like incense. In the direction of her door, Baboro slowly drew the sign of the cross in the air.

One by one they followed the seminarian, who had gone back to the kitchen to read his breviary. The kid was sent again. He reported that Il Nero was there, eavesdropping. He unexpectedly called him

84

by that name. Nothing could be heard; then, a thud. The stacked firewood was collapsing as it burned. Shortly after, Annaloro announced a groan. Four of them rushed out, but they came back with no news.

"Women groan," Annaloro said, resenting that no one was asking him for his expert explanations.

"Then they scream. Their screams give you the creeps."

"Do they scream a lot?" inquired Divinangelo, who had never found himself in a similar predicament.

And Annaloro, now reconciled: "They scream for hours."

The boy asked, "But why?" He was by the fireplace with the hen, in his usual position, with a knee on the step and his head thrust forward like a butting little goat.

Only Alleluia was quiet; he disdained to be troubled by a human female undergoing labor pains. Piglets slid out of his sows like eels, he had gathered up hundreds of them.

It got dark. Nobody thought about cooking something. Now and then they would cut a piece of bread and cheese, and take a bite while they stood around. Almost always it was the boy who would listen at the door and then come back with no news. They were looking at the seminarian, but he never lifted his eyes from the book. As he smoothed each one down with his closed fingers and shiny pink nails, the turning pages rustled like dry leaves. The men were all staring at those white hands, the black book, the clean nails, and the calm motion.

At ten, he got up and left the kitchen. They overheard his steps in the hallway. He stopped. Two light knocks on the door, then a third one, stronger. His voice. Vanzi's voice. He came back. Nothing we can do, she says everything is fine; she doesn't want to be disturbed. The men were dumbfounded, a deep dismay hung over their faces. It is not natural. That a woman silently gives birth and wants to stay alone by herself, locked in, this is not natural.

Once again the water stopped boiling above the ashes and Annaloro added more. Then he had the impression it was no longer clear; he threw it out, rinsed the cauldron, and hung it back on the chain by the fireplace. Fearing the water would not boil again soon enough, they put more branches and logs on the fire, stoked it and blew on it, raising the ash again.

Yawning, the boy said, "We should have shot her right away."

They avoided each other's eyes. Deaf and mute, the seminarian stood there, straight as a log. They had a grudge against him. They were dismayed and lost and he did not care. As if he had deliberately abandoned them. His support failed them, the confused idea that by virtue of his robe he could somehow avert the curse that hovered over the events. They were resentful, too, because he had failed to save her from the death sentence.

But when Baboro observed that the priest couldn't care about them, and that it made sense, they all nodded. The only innocent was the boy, and they were responsible for him as well. With peaceful abandon, he had finally fallen asleep on the bench. The hen was crouched down on his lap like a cat.

At midnight, Vanzi and Franzè reappeared; they too had not gone to bed. Pointing at the boy, Alleluia repeated that it was better to shoot her right away and Franzè agreed. Hehe, the men sniggered, but it all seemed artificial.

"Maybe," Divinangelo hazarded, "she dies alone."

"What, what do you mean alone?"

"She dies in there giving birth. Maybe she's dead already."

"She's dead?" Hoarse voices asked the seminarian as he came back from her door.

Nothing had changed; she did not want anyone to come in.

"Did she say that? She said something? What did she say?"

It turned out that she had not talked, but if anyone so much as touched the door, she would moan louder. What, she moans? She moaned, well, she groaned in her throat so she couldn't be heard. With all due respect, they recognized she was a courageous woman. And Annaloro said that without screaming and giving vent to her pain she really was risking her life. Women must scream, for God's sake.

Suddenly they all turned on Franzè for sending back the wives. Menina had wanted to stay, she had begged and railed on and on and cried to stay there, she said they would go mad alone, they would let her die. Shooting her is one thing, we are trapped and war makes men cruel, but letting her die like a dog . . . . They were shouting hoarsely and could hardly recognize their own voices as they raised and waved their hands. There they were, going mad for real. Until Vanzi, whirling his arm, seemed to cut off the whole chorus.

The boy was still sleeping on the bench, all rosy, just like the little angel he was.

6. Once more the priest went to her. They followed, one by one. In the freezing dark of the hallway, they leaned against the wall to listen, each with a desolate expression. A deep growl, like the rage of an animal, was coming from inside. It lasted an eternity. When it stopped, their faces were pale and distressed. The young man knocked, first lightly with his knuckles, then loud, then louder, insistently, with his fist.

"Let me in," he begged. "I can do something for you, help you out. Do you want old Baboro to come in?" He slightly pulled out the latch bolt.

"Go away," a choked, unrecognizable voice replied. "If you come in, I . . ." And the growl started again.

The young man dropped his arms along the sides of his cassock, and froze. Then suddenly he fell to his knees, holding the crucifix with both hands and moving his lips to pray. It wasn't clear whether he was pleading for her life or her death. A fierce breathing penetrated the walls and their ears, it really made the men go mad. The groan, the open cry of their wives had never been so piercing and charged with dark omens. Even Alleluia, feeling confused, was grinding his sharp teeth.

Annaloro said, "Those are the tossing labor pains. And she doesn't even have a headboard to cling to for support."

No one could say how long it went on. Then a cry, a single cry, that gave them all the creeps. It was dawn. Silence reigned, even more upsetting. She is dead. And all at once, unexpectedly, a shriek. Like a bird landing. The shriek was repeated three times, irrefutable. The young man immediately grabbed the bolt and pulled it out, but did not open the door.

He got an answer to his timid query. "Wait, I will call."

It was, for Christ's sake, her voice. Completely natural.

Annaloro, coming around, rushed to get the cauldron and put it down between their legs. Someone asked, "What is he doing?" But nobody paid attention to him; they were craning their necks. Time had stopped again. When the priest opened the door, nobody had heard a sound. He entered alone, leaving the door half-closed; no one dared to push it further. They caught a glimpse of the dying embers in the fireplace, two uncovered pots on the ground, close by a cotton tuft, rosy as if the fire could be seen through it. And the whitish back of the little chair, crosswise.

"She wants Annaloro," the young man said rushing out with a bundle in his arms.

Annaloro went in without the cauldron. The others followed the priest in the kitchen. He was holding, wrapped tightly in a woolen cloth, the newborn baby.

"She said I have to keep it warm."

They were upset because of the way he was talking, bewildered and vulnerable, just like one of them. Alleluia and Divinangelo fed the fire, raising the flames. The boy got up from the bench, yawning and stretching. He saw the bundle on the priest's lap and leaned out and asked, "What is it?" But his hen, flying next to him, clucking, immediately distracted him. The men, exhausted as if they had delivered too, were staring in silence as they gathered around the bench where the young man was rigidly sitting. He was still carefully holding the bundle against his cassock.

As Annaloro came back, they looked up at him anxiously. He was carrying an armful of linens, and immersed them in a bucket filled with water, pressing them down with his hands and producing a gurgle like the sound of someone drowning.

"She did everything by herself," he burst out. "What a great woman. She was lying down and all of this holy mess was gathered under her bed, not a single drop could be seen. Like the female cats that lick everything and you find them all clean and tidied up. She says she wants to sleep. She says we have to keep the baby warm."

The boy got closer and looked in the bucket. "Is that blood?" Then he saw the scissors; he probably thought they were used to open the womb during delivery. Annaloro pushed him away and the hen shrieked.

And made the announcement: "It's a baby girl."

The seminarian relaxed his grip. Between the edges of the blanket, a clean, tidy white face appeared under a fuzz of hair. It was a full head of black hair, unusually thick, dark and long for a newborn. And her eyes were open; round, vivid, small eyes, just like a bird's. They seemed to see, to observe with severity the men surrounding her, their bashful and shamefaced welcome. The men who intended to kill her mother. They looked away.

Baboro made a hasty sign of the cross on his chest, as if lightning had flashed.

The hen had been flapping and emitting sharp clucks that everybody ignored. The boy, with her always on his shoulder, sneaked in and leaned over to see the baby. He seemed to meet those small eyes and stared at them; suspicious, annoyed, with a visceral malevolence and disgust. He was holding something in his hand. He showed it. An egg. The just-laid egg of his young hen. He held it under each one's nose, proudly. The egg was small, with a tender shell, variegated with bloody, virginal streaks.

The young man seemed to be speechless, but he still could speak as a priest. In a loud voice he asked for water and salt. Scattered around the kitchen, kneeling down, they all witnessed the baptism.

VIII

1. Once you start climbing, there's no turning back. The rubber boot cracks the icy crust with each step and gets stuck. Even so, you have to take the risk and lift the next leg and let it sink. When he reaches the last step he's drenched in sweat and sends out a plume of breath between his lips. Then he stands there, exhaling little clouds, and blowing them up to the sky, but the whiteness that surrounds him absorbs everything instantly. All is a dazzling whiteness, huge white horses are bucking over the horizon.

Stomping his feet, with his hands stuck in his pockets, he cautiously goes toward the church door. Inside, it's freezing too. The bare rocks, the loose stones, even the crumbling altar with its two broken steps exhale a freezing breath. He wanders around, continuing to stomp his feet; he doesn't want to run. Down in the monastery, there's the fireplace, but the murderers are there, too. He grinds his little teeth. He hates them with all his growing strength. He is strong — his neck cords are tense, his body completely stiff — he feels as if he could kill them all. For not only did they drain off the blood . . . ah, they even licked the delicate bones. That woman may have drank all the broth, but they, they have been sucking the bones — disgusting. Oh, and they even tried to hide it; Divinangelo buried the feathers under the snow. My little Conchita. He feels like crying.

A young pullet—*primipara*, they said—and its first, nice, little egg. And many more were ready and waiting inside, in sequence like an amber necklace, all yolks, and Alleluia was savoring the raw eggs, dripping with blood. The swine.

Circling, his hands still in his pockets, still stomping, he holds back his tears and despises them more than ever. They're turning into sissies, all sappy around those two females. Didn't Franzè himself want to climb up to the Rapina—risking his life with the hungry wolves—to ask the Germans for disinfectant and gauzes? And then old Baboro, who insists on going to the farm because she needs some ointment. Ointment for the red bottom of the frog. They wag their tails around her bed, one with the herb tea, another with the broth—even the coffee, once—another one asking if she needs anything else. And Annaloro keeps scrubbing the disgusting bloodstained linens. The priest never lets go, even for a moment, of the bundle, he cuddles it and once gave it his finger to suck. What has gotten into them? No, I will never sleep next to Divinangelo again, he stinks.

He feels rejected. He runs off crying. He cries for himself, his Conchita, the whole world infested by men. And just a little later, while he sits on the altar steps—facing backward, he confusedly crosses himself, just in case—he imagines big hens with soft, enormous breasts filling the earth. Only hens, all around him, pecking at his earlobes, petting him with their wings, and brushing his neck with their feathers. They have such arched, high, light, and feathered breasts. Not like women. He hates women, from the treacherous house servants to this one here; her veined breast, repulsively dangling loose when she breastfeeds, while all the men watch. He prefers himself, the little keyboard of his ribs, his tender little thighs, and his sensitive groin.

He is freezing again. He walks and stomps again in gloomy dereliction. An orphan. For the first time he calls himself that and suffers. The frog still has her mother (he never even met his), she has the men looking after her, and she had Conchita; the pullet was sacrificed for her. No, I won't cry, they must not see me whining, I won't cry, not even now when I'm alone. And so there, clenching his fists, he loses his sweet childish frailty. His throat hurts, eh. But now he is too proud and hard inside to abandon himself to tears.

In the end, he is irresistibly drawn to the choir. That place. The central choir stall is for the leader. He sits rigidly, stretching his arms out straight from both sides, wearing his prickly wool hat tall as a miter, and his little neck sticking up from his frayed sweater. He says, "You can't." Around him are the men: spineless, idle, and silent. Ah, he knows well what is wrong with them: they lost their strength. He feels a reckless giddiness.

"You can't!" he shouts. "You can't change your minds!"

His father, the house, and the fire—he doesn't remember them clearly, like being in a fog. Everything leaves, recedes, flees back into the distance, and disappears. Only Divinangelo's stinking shirt is close at nighttime. But from now on I will sleep on the bench. He feels confused; he doesn't know why he is there with them. C'mon, you have to shake the dirt off your shoes—the shoes are made of pigskin—and march forward, death to the traitors. Who was the betrayer? No, it was set on fire. But why? The flaming tongues lick away, the bluebottle explodes. His scars slightly ache. The fire leaves its mark. We are faithful to the idea . . . ah we are heroes . . . . It's impossible to remember everything the men said, their big words. Now they behave like good husbands and cradle the little daughter. She is not an orphan.

"I object!" he cruelly shouts toward the stalls.

He hasn't seen me.

But was I there? Maybe I wasn't.

Today, forty years later, copying these old papers and putting the pieces together, I realize I have always faced other men as a spectator, but with the boy I felt an identification. As if I were he, my child self.

Or was it just a literary exercise?

2. "This baby will live. We both easily could have died during that night. But now I know that she will survive. Once you brought her back to me, I looked at her and I could see the resemblance. Not that I remember my mother's face very well. But I immediately saw the resemblance. Here is that same frowning, patient expression again, that tenacity toward life. I feel great pity for her. I've given birth to two other children. They died as babies, I can't even remember their faces. But this one will survive.

"Listen, it's not like they say, I've never been a whore, I've borne men's children. Is that the same to you? You are subtle and yet you don't make distinctions. So you want her. Of course you do. Since the first day you've wanted her. As if I were not forced by the situation to leave her in your hands. Who would take her otherwise? Besides, maybe they aren't still planning to kill me. The old man said—he always pontificates—'If you, woman, have something sacred on which you can swear . . .' Maybe they will change their minds about it. I do have, yes, something sacred, but for that same reason I can't swear on it. You insinuate that I don't want to be saved. But you don't want that, either, hehe. Maybe you will get my confession—in a way, you already have it—but you couldn't use it anyway. Alright, you won't talk, I know. Those men are waiting for me to regain my strength. You, though, are waiting for me to grow weak. I am weak, in fact. I am even scared. When I wake up, I come around with a start, I make the sign of the cross under the blankets and beg: Oh god, my god. The little animal raised in the tenements wakes up. But I wake up too, right away. Sometimes I take my pulse; if I can't find it or it's not regular, I'm breathless, I feel nauseous. It's the breastfeeding. It sucks me out.

"C'mon, don't call me sister, and don't tell me you're always waiting. When you slip back into your role you get unctuous. Besides, I can't treat you like I did before. Not you or the others. Living with the enemy is a mistake; you knew that and counted on it. As the boy understood, they should have killed me right away. And Il Nero knew that too. In his own way he's got it together, that is, he's consistent. You too. You have become my nightmare, in my dreams I see a calf's head by my bedside with your meek and patient eye. But I am smart too. In opposing fields, we're both champions. (That Vanzi is a waste of talent; he hasn't got a field anymore.) You thought about that, didn't you? And obviously you believe you're going to win. Even afterward, when you leave with the child, you'll think you have won. Is that so? Bah, you never say anything straight out, you never come right out with it. But I think I actually will win if you can leave with the child. That is, if I will be dead.

"You will hand over the notebook. It is a small notebook; it won't take too much space. I will give it to you at the end. I will give you a letter. But you'll have to memorize the address and then forget it. I authorize you to talk, to tell everything—no names, alright?—so that people will know. Yes, all my ambitions are here, on earth. It's all here. I could have been someone. Ah, I had so many ambitions. And I end up like this. These drifters will get rid of me in a rush; they will put me in a hole and run away. People must know, my papers must reach their destination, there is something there . . . . I've had ideas, a lot of ideas. And the prisoner's final hours . . . but I have no strength anymore, you will tell everything. And not just hours . . . a long torture . . . . Their hesitations and your tenacity will draw it out even longer. I could have written . . . . But even in this form it's going to be a document. It's no use you reading it; in fact, I forbid you, you have to swear you won't. Someone will edit out the errors, there must be heaps of them, it doesn't matter. I am telling you . . . you hand that over and that's all. I give you the child. I don't even ask you what you are going to do with her, I know perfectly well what your plans will be for her. But you won't succeed; she has good blood running in her veins. I think I have not wasted the short time I've had, I leave a life behind, a sequel.

"Well, yes, I did kill Baborino. In another village, it's just the same. Like here, we were in the mountains. After that episode I switched territories and came to operate in this area. I had to kill. But you already knew that, because I've also told you about it in my dream, I've told the calf's head in the dream. It's no big deal for me to say it face-to-face. This is what you were waiting for, eh? So, his donkey sidled up to my donkey, my little jenny, and started hopping around her. His donkey wanted to mount her even with all her bundles. We both beat him on the backside with our axe handles, but the donkey was set on it. And then the bundles moved and the peasant saw the weapons. He didn't realize what he was seeing at first, he was staring dumbfounded. He had lowered his axe, puzzled by the situation. But I knew he would understand, eventually. So I had no choice. A massive neck, a big red head like Alleluia's. I raised my axe and struck it down on that big head. He had no time to realize, and didn't put up any defense, he was already half-gone. And still standing, he didn't protect himself, his arms were already useless. And I hit him like a tree, I hit him hard, he collapsed. He was not dead. One of his eyelids was cut, and out of that crack he was looking at me with a red and blue eye. I had to hit his head over and over until it broke. I was hitting him the way you do when you find a knot in the grain of a log, I was hitting hard and ferociously.

"I should have done the same with Franzè. He was astonished, too, the rifle over his shoulder, as he faced a pregnant woman, without a clue. He doesn't know the risk he ran. But I still had that cracked-open eye in front of me. I can see it now. When that boorish Alleluia looks at me, I can see it in the middle of his forehead. My nerves aren't the nerves I used to have, otherwise how could I sit here and talk about it? The thing had been really nasty. But what else could I have done? Even if they don't like it, these people, too, have no choice. They should have hurried up, like I did. It was a hideous crime that was blamed on the Germans and stirred up hatred. And that was a good thing. I pay the price; things add up. You think that things should add up differently, that I should feel some remorse. I couldn't have acted otherwise, can you understand this? Right, you can't. In the service of a cause, scruples and remorse are abandoned. You do know that. But of course you would like to know who guarantees the righteousness of the cause. Eh, who? No, not God, obviously. We don't want God to be our guarantor, like hypocrites do. *Gott mit uns*, everybody uses that as a shield. We want to go ahead without it, I've already explained that. Clinging to tradition in order to survive: this is what you do. But in order to live, you need to break away from tradition. To cut the umbilical cord. I've cut it with my own hands. I know I know, you felt your guts ripped out that night, too. You always try to lead me astray and maybe move me with those eyes. Alright, you have been human. But the problem is that we need to turn all mankind human. Don't ask me to repent. You will never break me down to that point. I mean, in your own way, you think you can make me stronger. Even though we speak different languages, I understand yours. But you can't understand mine. You are battling against me, you know? Battling with an exhausted woman. I can see you with the calf's head again, the enormous eye, patient, disgustingly meek. Enough, eh? When I see you like that, I have to stop. Enough, go away now, leave."

3. They went to the church after midnight, when the snow started falling again. The boy seemed to be asleep; they left him curled up on the bench. But he immediately got up. Wearing the big fur hat he never took off, not even to go to bed (he will get ringworm, the others said), he ran barefoot across the kitchen. He didn't waste time wearing socks and tying shoes; he simply thrust his feet in the boots abandoned in a corner. Paying me no mind, he set out on silent rubber soles. On his way he made sure that the prisoner's door was well locked from the outside, and gave the latch a hard push. A

wail could be heard inside. Humming prayers drifted from the seminarian's cell. He had been deliberately excluded and the latch to his door pulled shut for the first time. I was left out, too, for I had never accepted a weapon. I didn't know how to shoot.

I followed the kid. Entering by what was once the sacristy, we went inside the church behind the choir. They were sitting in the stalls like the last time and their voices resounded. They didn't, or maybe they did, see us while we were sneaking along the wall to get to the altar and then, moving around it, reach the steps. The low altar wall hid us, even though it had crumbled. From the corner we could glimpse what was going on and listen. We were the audience. Half hidden.

The kid, sitting on the first step, eventually turned over and kneeled down. At a slant, as if he were eavesdropping behind a door, he was all bent over to relieve the pain of his legs wrapped in their tight boots. They reached up to his thighs and bit into the backs of his knees. He suffered the whole time.

At first the voices were dispersed in the void and impossible to make out. But gradually, words could be distinguished, the tone of the voices grew louder. Vanzi again proposed, in a curt voice, the death sentence. He was sitting in the prior's central stall, Franzè at his right, then Divinangelo, and next Alleluia. At his left, representing the minority view, were Baboro and Annaloro, who had asked for an appeal. It looked like it was already over. Franzè stood up, ready to go.

But Baboro now demands proof. Why, the weapons are not proof? And what about the fire? People have been killed. Baboro, old fool, his son has been massacred and he still questions the sentence. He would like to save her—bloody hell! The kid was listening while he shifted on his bent knees, a hand over his mouth. He let out a gurgle. He wiped his hand on his trousers, for he must have been drooling.

The discussion had heated up. Their voices overlapped and blurred in the echoing vault. And feet were thumping, rifles clanging, the wooden stalls and benches creaking. The kid was restless, lifting his head and shoulders, opening and closing his mouth — as everybody does, spurring his teammates, when pick-up games are held in the village square. He was eloquent, but voiceless. C'mon, c'mon Franzè, attack, attack him. Baboro, you old, docile blockhead, should I pardon her for killing my father? They've all grown weak. They've lost their courage. There's no way out, eh, boss? No turning back. We have to damn ourselves to hell. What a word! Let's damn ourselves. He whispered that word again, crouching down until his forehead touched the third step. And then, louder: c'mon c'mon, do it.

On both sides of the low wall, as if through two lateral eyes, dim halos of fading light could be glimpsed. The men, with only their pale foreheads visible, were black shadows in the hollows of the stalls. They stepped down to stand at attention, with their rifles straight up in the military style. And the first vote resounded, by voice and a show of hands. Vanzi and the two at his side: yes. Baboro and Annaloro: no. Four to two. It was still looking like a parody to me.

But the old man stubbornly protests. The commandment says: Thou shalt not kill. But what about letting yourself be killed? People have been killed. And more people will be killed. God also commands we must not let someone kill others. She will continue, she has refused to swear she'll stop. She is a soldier, knows the law of war, accepts it, and we, like sissies, are whining about whether we should carry out the sentence or not. Because we haven't got the courage to take up the rifle and shoot against a self-proclaimed enemy. We are defeated men; we lack even the courage of a defense. We are lost. We risk being shot by the Germans for hiding a partisan.

The kid has thrown himself completely across the step, stretching and parting his legs to bring some relief. He sighs. He lays his head on his arm and listens with one ear. It's Vanzi who is feebly defending the result of the vote, the legality of the sentence during wartime. Franzè gets excited and feels fired up. They must respect the vote.

Otherwise, he is ready to carry out the sentence by himself. No, the others protest: all together, side by side, it's a shared responsibility. We are all tied to a chain. Or is it just to egg each other on?

The kid is shivering as if he were repressing a laugh, shakes his head, twists back and forth. Next to him, I can see the others stuck side by side, their rifles oscillating in the air, their legs bending, like paper dolls hooked together. Paper arms. They won't shoot.

Suddenly Baboro raises his hand, points a finger. And Alleluia, unhooking the lamp from his stall, descends the squeaky platform and goes and hooks the lamp on the stall back closer to his master. He has moved to the other side. The long silence that follows is so deep that they clearly can hear the woodworms gnawing away, their vigorous drills in the choir's seasoned oak.

In that silence, like an explosion, the second poll: three to three. They all start talking at once in a hullabaloo of voices, echoes, and rumbles. Another vote follows right after, the vote is repeated, as if the count were difficult or the alignments had changed again. The vote is null. They won't arrive at a solution.

Vanzi stands up with a resolute gesture and imposes silence. The big bold head appears closer than it is, white as chalk, marked with that pitch black concealed in the curves of the plaster. And they each emerge below their foreheads; white faces marked with black. The lamps have in their sooty spouts nothing more than a yellowish clot, like spit. It's the dawn. It slightly brightens up through the dusty windows. Vague shadows of frescoes acquire a shade of color, while the faces are still intensely chalky.

So is this the end? It's daytime. It's important to get moving and go take a piss in the corner . . . over there . . . in that corner. To lift an arm, to stretch the legs, to move this numb arm. He slowly gets up from the steps, as rigid as if his body were made of wood. He walks crookedly as he comes before the choir. The men look at him in a daze. Under his rough fur miter, he stares at everybody with a harsh look. As for me, he had never looked at me, it was as if I were not there.

"I object," he shouts. "I was at the trial; I get to vote, too. She burned my father alive. I have the right to vote."

Walking crookedly, swallowed up to his groin in the boots, he stands before the men, his arm held up straight.

4. When they awakened, the little kitchen window was completely clogged with snow. At noon, it looked no lighter than dawn. Once the window was brushed clear, the light from outside seemed to swarm. A full heavy wave of snow from the coast was coming down with the east wind. The snow had settled on the ground, piling up in dunes. The kid plunged in with his boots. His wolf cub's cry died without an echo.

Alleluia was lighting the fire, thriftily piling logs in the fireplace. It would be a while before they could cut more firewood. The linden tea was announced. Annaloro had hung the cauldron and was dropping in fistfuls of the dried herb. Divinangelo saved a pinch of the floating stuff to fill his pipe. They needed to stop by the Rapina to get a supply of tobacco from the Germans; otherwise there would be no smoking on the trip back.

"Provided that the Germans have some," Franzè grumbled, lifting up the peaked cap on his whitened forehead. But he was afraid that the Germans were no longer at the Rapina.

"Oh yes, they have some," Divinangelo assured. "They get less snow from the coast. Beyond here not every place is buried."

"Beyond here," Baboro repeated in singsong.

Nobody was really thinking about that trip toward a mythical north. Let it snow, let the snow pile up. Until it falls everything is yet to be done. Someone observed under his breath that it was the first day of the year. In church, the night before, they had completely forgotten. Thanks to the snow! Hehe, they cackled.

"He who kills on New Year's Day," the old man decreed, "kills all year 'round."

Thanks to the snow, they would not kill on New Year's Day. Although, the priest would observe, they intended to. But after all, why saddle a man with his intentions when he can't even decide his own actions? The devil grabs your arm and leads it wherever he wants. He has put his tail here too, his forked tail. The smell of linden spread through the kitchen as it revived and puffed in the cauldron. The kid, coming in with the woman's bowl, sniffed the air and headed to the fireplace. From the open door came a wail. Shortly after, the seminarian appeared with his breviary. He took a peep at the window. The snow was whirling.

"Besides," Annaloro broke the silence, "we could not get her out of her bed so soon. It weakens the lower back. My first wife would lie down for ten days in a row. She was a skinny woman, but a wise one. She died, in fact." Looking around, he stopped talking.

The seminarian closed his breviary and went into the prisoner's cell. The poor thing, wrapped in the gray military blanket on the bed, was restless. The kid, squatting on his heels, was there stoking the fire. She was sitting on the little chair.

"What are you doing here?" the young man reproached him, frowning. But he laughed with the disarming innocence of a child.

"Don't scold him," the woman intervened. "We were talking about blowflies."

"Blowflies?"

"Bluebottle blowflies. Fire goblins. It's something between us." And abruptly: "Take him with you."

"But I am leaving with the men," the boy flared up at once.

When the baby wailed, the woman sat down on the hard edge of the bed, pulled her breast out and started breastfeeding. She had covered herself with a handkerchief like peasant women do.

"I," the boy reaffirmed at the doorstep, "I am staying with them."

Maybe he had forgotten his father, but not the burning urge for reprisal. He had told her everything.

"An innocent," the young man whispered.

"How ferocious innocence can be, a tiger. Innocence doesn't know mercy. And you have been the mute angel."

"I have not been allowed."

"But you also gave up trying. For that other Baborino, I know. God doesn't pay on Saturday, eh? Vengeance is up to him."

"You always want . . . I beg you, sister, let everything go, think that the moment is getting closer."

"When?"

"The men are relying on the snow to delay things. But if the skies clear up . . . . And you, sister, you are not ready."

"I am both prepared and ready. It's all set. Even the little cloths to be filled with sugar. She will suck them while you're on your journey. I will give you some of my milk as well, the last squeeze. Will I know it's coming beforehand?"

The child had fed at both breasts, and she tucked her into the blanket. Returning to her little chair, pressing her back with a sigh against the back of the chair, the woman stretched her big shoes out to the fire. "My back is wrecked," she said. "Forty years old, I'm not young anymore. I delivered my first baby, too, by myself, but I quickly recovered. I had to work. This is the first time I can laze around. These are luxuries one has to pay for."

"I," the seminarian rushed to say, "I can't find the words. I could not find any. I'm here in vain. I beg your pardon."

"No no, my young man, of course not! In fact you're the only man in a cassock I've ever been able to tolerate. You are a peasant, simple and realistic. You threw away all that trash for the confessional—or maybe you haven't yet mastered it, it doesn't matter—you instinctively realized it would be useless. I acknowledge your merit. Tomorrow our worlds will collide. But today I don't want to fight with you, let's leave that to the future. I thank you for everything; you were genuinely willing to help me. But you can't help me."

"Is this a farewell?"

"No, dear, I am not dismissing you. Come again, if you want. Here is the baby, she is yours. I will entrust you with the papers. And now go and take a rest. You've been up all night to pray, eh? Maybe in the middle of the floor, kneeling down. There's still the mark of that, your cassock is too black. Me, take a rest? I will have plenty of time afterward. Eh, dear, I will be watching through the window bars. The boy said it's possible to see quite a few stars. Maybe I will see them tonight."

5. The night a stable boy from the farmhouse arrived, stamping off the mud that was up to his knees, the mood was almost festive. He was carrying two flasks of wine and two big rounds of cheese; they drank and ate their fill. He had come to deliver a message from the village to Vanzi; nobody seemed to be curious about it. As if they wanted to ignore it. The stable boy slept on one of the benches in the kitchen, with the other kid on the other bench scowling at him. By dawn he had left. Franzè immediately sent an order to clear the snow in the churchyard.

There hadn't been any snow for the past four days. A crystalline sky stretched in a great curve and the surrounding whiteness seemed to curdle as if it had been stirred. But the wind blowing in from the mountain, the icy wind that bites noses and cheeks, was like a glass wall. Cracking the frozen crust at every step, with their heads down to protect their faces, the men took to their hard work. They started pitching the snow down the slope, clearing out a stony path that could lead to the rock face. The mountain's vertical, steep, cracked face, with lumps of snow that seemed to bloom in the crevices. Using a spatula from the kitchen, the boy joined in with the others as they shoveled. He was lively and talkative, but couldn't get a word out of the men. Franzè supervised and lent a hand himself through all the shifts. Vanzi often went out to check on things. The priest was nowhere to be seen.

In the kitchen knocking together a meal, Annaloro had dropped potato skins all over the ground, dirty dishes in the sink, and a lidless cauldron smack in the middle of the floor. Old Baboro was dozing off on the bench, ignoring the fire as it faded away. After lunch, muddy footprints and puddles of melted snow formed black spots, leaving a trail from the entrance to the hallway. A white mush of snow and ashes was piled near the fireplace. Two socks with pigskin soles were hanging from the mantel to dry. One sock fell into the fire and slowly burned, filling the air with the revolting smell of singed wool. Vanzi, turning up his nose, removed it from the half-extinguished embers. He stood there for a while then wandered around in the kitchen. Again he stopped in front of the soaked, smoke-colored panties left from the wives' visit — they were hanging across the back of the gutted chair, their laces dripping.

Later the seminarian walked in and headed to the fireplace, where he stirred the fire and added new logs. He rummaged through the cabinet. There was the little bit of sugar left for the baby, nobody had touched it. And some leftover coffee beans. He had to grind them in the salt mortar, then dropped a few pinches in the coffeepot and boiled it, the way friars do. While the coffee was still steaming, he picked it up with the sugar and didn't give a single glance to the filthy mess around him.

Exhausted and wet, the men came back in, sniffing the vague nostalgic smell of coffee in that unwelcoming camp kitchen. Through the small window, not yet frosted, the intense complexion of the sky brightened. The sunset had been blazing; the last mass of clouds — high, puffy, and soft, had almost disappeared behind the crest, lit by a pink fire. The snow was as pink as oleander flowers and the mountains wore their forests like a curly violet mane.

Again the cauldron was set on the fire for the potatoes. Annaloro was frying some rancid lard. With troubled faces, the men waited for the soup to be ready. Divinangelo was whining about his burnt sock. Franzè nervously looked for another place to dry his still-soaked panties. Only the boy was moving about, lively and at ease amid the garbage and the dampness. Two or three times he declared he was hungry. But no one paid him any attention, and he went out again to scan the weather.

There was always that mass of clouds on the horizon, not yet swallowed up and extinguished. The sky seemed ash gray, the trampled snow pearl gray, all the white was suddenly opaque, and the ragged edge of the woods turned black. And out there the kid, too, was transformed, shrunken back into a small child, looking scorched and yellow, withered. How come? It's changing for the worse again. But shortly after the leaden instant that follows twilight, the sky gave way to a shining transparent evening. The first star pulsed on the surface, the night's deep blue thickened and intensified. All the faint noises of the clear rigid night: the crackling of the thinnest branches, a fluttering like small hard-shelled insects, the soft thudding sound of mysterious fallings. And there the boy, freezing, stood very still with a dreamy expression on his face. That night, for the second time, he took my hand and let himself be brought back inside.

They had dinner around the fireplace, with just one lamp on the mantelpiece that flickered and sent out a dim glimmer within the red glow coming from the flames. The shovelers, their feet still soaked with the snow and their bodies exhausted, ate with no appetite. When Vanzi appeared, they all turned their heads, and at once bent back again over their bowls. He looked obstinate, even worse than the boy. Heads down, chewing their cud, they felt a deep sharp hatred toward him.

The convicted prisoner and the priest had received their rations in their cells, but shortly after, the priest walked in. And again they felt forced to look out of the corners of their eyes in suspicion. This is the way, resolute and relentless, that priests move inside houses when someone is dying. They were pleased to notice he had some red spots on his neck and toward the bottom of his cheeks.

And then, all at once, they handed themselves over to him.

Baboro was the first. "Father Don Antonino, pray for us tonight."

He assured them he would pray for everybody and resolutely asked to take the boy away with him. They unanimously agreed. Sure. It's right. Obviously. We have to leave the boy to him. It seemed inexplicable that they could have gotten into such an adventure, one that now seemed meaningless, aberrant, and ultimately criminal. They were submissive, annihilated. There, sleeping like a little angel, was the boy. They would hand the boy to him, sure. Yes, we'll let the boy go and we'll leave this place without him. It was as if he were abandoning them irreversibly, enlisting them among the lost.

"Will you head toward the Rapina?" the priest asked in an uninterested tone.

The Rapina? Eh, maybe, who knows. Exacerbated voices. If it's frozen, the snow will be as hard as stone. And besides, why should they go to the Rapina? They will go, the devil knows where.

6. The woman was roaming the narrow space of her cell as if it were a cage. She lifted her dazed eyes.

"I haven't seen you in a while," she said wryly. And took up her pacing again, dodging the corner of the bed. "Go ahead, come on, it's tomorrow?"

"Tomorrow."

"What time?"

"They are deciding."

She had poured what remained of the coffee into the pot kept warm by the embers. She drank a little of it and started pacing again. She took out her comb and put it back repeatedly; long stray locks hung down her neck. Straight, as if they had lost their vitality.

"It shakes my nerves but holds them up. I will drink it bitter, instead of vinegar and bile. Now I'm worked up, but later I will be very calm. I will die well. You didn't think you'd turn me to salt with your announcement, did you? I knew it, I've always known, I never really deluded myself. And I never counted on my comrades to rescue me. They were about to cross the lines, they have ignored my fate. The only solution would have been to drop dead that night with the baby. Because it does bother me, I swear it bothers me, although the word might seem ridiculous. If you are going to drown, better in a sea than a puddle."

She felt a strong surge of rebellion, clapping her hands on her thighs and clawing at her skirt as if she could rip her own skin off.

"To die at the hands of these poor drifters, people who don't even know why they're fighting. Ah, and caught like an animal that by chance landed right in the hunter's lap. We stumbled into each other, ha-ha. And people used to always say of me: this woman, she can hear the grass grow. And so tomorrow I will be dead. Dead, you see. Everything will be over for me. For me only. Right when it was just beginning. And I will be shut out of it forever. Now, now that I was enjoying being in the world. I was enjoying it enormously, passionately, I tell you. I had left the ditch and I know that anyone and everyone can leave and I wanted to help them do it.

"So, I have to go. They will thrust me in a hole, I'll be back in a ditch. Tomorrow, tomorrow by daytime, they'll rule my destiny, they'll wipe me out. Eh? Away, away, forever. Don't even think of convincing me with your stories. I will spend the whole night staring at the stars behind the bars — you can see two or three stars — thinking that I will never see them again. Go ahead and hope — I can read that on your face — that they will speak to me about God. Well, hope for it, if you like it. Anyway, they will surely speak to me, they will pierce me and tear me to pieces. Our commotion lends words — of joy or sorrow, it doesn't matter — to silent nature. We're the only ones here and we're alone.

"I'll write it down. But no, how could I? I can't find words anymore . . . . Suddenly the meaning gets out of hand, everything that had seemed clear and incontrovertible . . . . Death. This death, oh. Why, but why? Yes yes, a Baborino. Him, eh? Always him. It took only a moment to break his head. And what did that peasant boy have in his mind, after all? I, I do have something inside my head . . . . I have been tortured for days and days. You can be on the point of death and languish out of fear, pure and simple instinctive fear, the fear of the animal under the stick. Another one . . . no, it's not just fear, it's not that fear. It's an atrocious surge . . . people say labor pains are jolting . . . this is jolting. A craving for living, for acting, for killing, yes, that too . . . craving for seeing, seeing the next day . . . ah, and I won't be here. I won't be here tomorrow to see the sun at noon beaming on the softened snow and none of you will pay any attention to that. I won't be here when this area will be liberated, or afterward. After that, only after that will there be a real beginning. And as for me, I was a woman of the future . . . I'm being robbed of my own tomorrow. I've heard them wailing and whining by the fireplace: one is sighing for his house, another for his field or his shop, another for his village and even the Fatherland. The Fatherland, wails that ridiculous Fascist. They know nothing, poor imbeciles. This is just the beginning. The world will be born again tomorrow. And these people kill me, a citizen of that new world. And they are not aware of that. Worst of all: they don't even know who I am but they have the power to kill me. They will kill me.

"Ah, I should strangle the little snake, that bad, rotten sprout. It was him, him. Eh, what are you doing now? I should have expected that. Where were you hiding that? But sure, every priest keeps a crucifix under his cassock, and hands it out to the children to kiss. No need to put it under my nose. I understand, yes, yes, it was not the boy's fault. God doesn't pay on Saturday, I know it by heart. Vengeance is His. After all, that's fine, those of us who die will pay up and close the account. You can't score other points? Well, Christ on the cross is eloquent enough. I bow to Him. Yes, I prostrate myself. But not before all of you. You have all betrayed Him. (I'm not saying you yourself, not you, kid). This is not what he wanted. And, watch it, I'm not talking about me. I'm talking about mankind. Mankind has been bamboozled. Or maybe mankind cheated. The earth is not small, but it is no match for the enormity of man's greed. The earth must finally become large enough for everyone. It's simple enough and tomorrow it will be done. Tomorrow . . . I will have enough earth to cover a grave. Oh, do something. Why are you just stiffly standing there? You could have saved me, you, the men themselves are scared to death. No, don't say it, calf-headed monster. Don't say you were here to save my soul. Don't say it, eh? Don't you dare. I want to save this body, this ugly, stinking body that has served me so well that I could carry it up the mountains, subject it to any stress, fill it up on food, make it tremble when I make love, squeeze new lives from it — make it flexible and powerful out of love for all mankind. Yes, this horrible female being that is in front of you loves mankind more than all of you. All of mankind, you included. And if I really felt like licking your teeth, I could have done that, too, out of a passion for nature and bitten you just like I would bite a fruit. Revolution too is obscene and bloody because of love. It is fanatical because of love. Revolution is a woman, it gives birth by itself the way I did. Ha-ha, I am the revolution. You saw that, and that's why you have not wanted to save me, I know. Vengeance is yours.

"I've made my scene. Well, go now. The show is over. You'll have the last one tomorrow."

110

IX

1. There had been a long silence. When the newborn wailed, she picked her up and started to feed her. Past the open door, the men shuffled their feet but didn't turn their heads. They had been hanging around and now were heading to their cells for the last night's sleep.

"They won't be able to sleep," she said quietly. She was calm, her face was relaxed and a little drawn, like the face of a convalescent. Holding the handkerchief against her breast, she was looking at the young man.

He was rigid, lacing his hands together so tightly that his fingertips had turned pale. Suddenly he asked her for forgiveness, in a whisper, like a guilty boy who has been caught in the act.

She gives him a motherly look, moved to pity. "You feel this torture too, eh? But all this damned mess has taught you more than the seminary and the years you spent in the confessional. Isn't that so? Now you are ready to enter the fray. And fancy that, I have prepared you."

"But I could not prepare you for your death . . . for a Christian death. Here, I will leave you the crucifix. I am going to the church. I will get down on my knees and pray. That's all I know how to do."

"There is undoubtedly a great power in . . . in this." She ran her fingers lightly over the cross.

While she was speaking, her chest heaved and her nipple slipped out of the baby's mouth, leaving her floundering. Opening her strong hand, she firmly returned the little head to her breast. The baby's head was full of black hair, a little like the hair of an animal, like a cat's, and it was as if she were breastfeeding some fruit of nature.

As he moved toward the door, she stopped him. "Wait, I want to tell you something more." She laughed in a friendly way. "Such a boy and so knowing . . . Don't get too proud, c'mon. Like the dove and like the snake. You have been quite a serpent, too. With your story about how God does not pay on Saturday you have rubbed some salt in the wound and never washed it out. You are a clean sword, I have to admit. You, young people; youth is a straight arrow. But it is true that as you age you lose the thread. You get rusty. We don't, we cut down to the bone until the end. C'mon, don't be offended by the violent metaphors; I am quoting from your scriptures. What do you think?"

The young man had not talked; he had just opened his mouth as if he were gasping for air.

It was she who resumed the subject; she was the one who needed to talk. "And I tell you that we firmly believe . . . . Like you two thousand years ago. You are not at the start anymore and that's a drawback, your work has come to an end. Or has it been betrayed? Well, it's still useful. A helpful tool but not a very effective one anymore. Anyhow, you know how much it still works — men are weak, scared, they fear the specter of death — how much power you all have. How powerful faith is, it can move mountains. We, too, intend to move mountains and wipe out the world's selfishness. Christ's love hasn't succeeded because it demands too much love. We intend to treat men harshly instead, even though we love them, or rather it's exactly because of that love: we have to treat them that way, we'd be in trouble if we indulged them. No more indulgence, not for a long time. Ah, I would like to live fifty more years, maybe it would be long enough. To see the Apocalypse, maybe. And why not a hundred, a thousand? When you're a beggar, wishing for a hundred or a thousand years is all the same. And I am so poor; I have but a few hours. Alas, I've just had to suffer this singular and authentic poverty: to have my very hours be numbered. Once again I digress. This is logorrhea. You can boast that you made me talk. Even I have lost interest in what I'm saying."

She caught her breath as if she were panting. They both seemed out of breath. The poor child had fallen asleep. She placed the baby on her knees and, prudishly turning to one side, laced up her bodice again.

Then she brusquely turned back. "You'd better go to bed. But look in the kitchen for that little aluminum canteen with the screw top. Not for the coffee, I'll go ahead and drink these dregs before. I'll have to pump milk at the last minute. I have as much milk as a cow. Otherwise the baby will drive you crazy on the way. Is it true that you will leave right after? The kid told me. He always comes and tells me everything. He declared: 'After we have gotten rid of you.' And boasting about it. He wants to be the center of attention."

"I will leave right away. They agreed to leave the boy to me. He thinks he is going with the men. But even if I have to tie him up . . . ."

"Tie him up then."

"I will head toward the sheepfolds. They will give me some fresh milk."

"Halfway you will give her mine. Don't forget to warm it up a little. You'll set her to sucking the little sugar mush every now and then; it kills hunger. She is famished, she wants to live. I will hand you everything in time, the papers too. Take the canteen and wash it thoroughly, the milk can easily turn sour. And dilute the sheep's milk with a little bit of fresh snow, it is too heavy."

They were speaking in a conversational tone, with the child in the middle, like two family members sharing advice about their household.

113

2. In the heart of the night uneasy shadows still roamed silently. The men could not get to sleep; it was as if they were spying, or spying on each other. Finally a heavy silence fell. The boy, in the kitchen, was sleeping the deep sleep of the innocent.

When everything was quiet, the seminarian tiptoed in. He hesitated, as if he did not know what to do. Then he headed with determination toward the canteen hanging from a nail and grabbed it. While he was busy scrubbing it, the woman came up behind his shoulder and he was startled.

"They forgot to lock me in." She laughed with a hand before her mouth in her typical peasant girl gesture. "Nobody is on guard duty; only our sleepless schoolteacher is around, omnipresent and unarmed. And I have looked outside. Drip the canteen well, like that. Look at the kitchen, a sty. They are demoralized. Bah, poor devils."

Gently the young man was pushing her toward the hallway, afraid that the boy could wake up.

"It's really freezing cold," she continued with a sort of excitement. "The cold could take off your very skin. A starry sky that crunches. The sky is a pane of glass, the stars are screeching against it, and it will break into pieces. The sky itself is weeping and gnashing its teeth. The churchyard is clear and ready for what's required. I haven't seen my grave. Where is it?"

Blocking her exit, the seminarian was trying to stop her. She seemed drunk: the effect of real coffee after years of substitutes. He asked, "Did you drink it all?"

"All. I drugged myself." She was laughing and pushing to go out. "But c'mon, you already want to bring me back to my cage. A sky like this . . . people around here say that whatever has not rained down is still in the sky. It should come down in pieces until mankind is submerged—a biblical solution. I could have run away, their heads have turned to mush. Maybe their hands will tremble and they will pierce me through too low. But my back is broken, a weight pulls me down, as if something inside is about to come loose. I never would have made it. Shall we go?"

He tried to resist. The woman was leaning against him and grabbing him by the arm, and begged: "Take me out for a moment. C'mon, it's no big deal. I couldn't sleep anyway, I feel drunk. And my night will be sucked dry. C'mon, it's important, I have to see the sky one more time. The ice has frosted my little window, it's sealed closed. No stars can be seen. Thank you, dear."

They walked with short steps, the woman dragging her feet as if one side were gone. There was no wind, but the crisp air chilled their clothes and harshly bit their faces. Over a white, slaked world—in front of the tall black outline of the cross—in the glass-sky the innumerable huge stars were throbbing.

Looking up, the priest dared to say passionately: "I beg you to repent, my sister."

There was no answer. She was looking up, too.

"It is . . . It's the stars," he was stuttering, "it is God up there" almost ashamed.

The woman held his arm tightly, as if lowering her head had upset her balance. And she started talking with an unusually guttural voice.

"You think I would not like that . . . . Ah, that would be so simple and soothing. But that's not possible. He would not want me at this point" she tittered. "It's no longer possible, we've burned our bridges. We put the massacre between us. I put an innocent Baborino between us." She whispered into her fingers, leaning as if she were spitting blood. And then stared again at him, intensely. "But the umbilical cord has been cut and we have to live and die alone. Maybe I will be forgiven, my brother. You cannot understand, but maybe I will be forgiven."

Her teeth were chattering. Slowly, dragging his feet to keep pace with hers, he brought her back inside.

The night was half over, the sky was high and sparkling.

115

3. At dawn, Franzè and Divinangelo went out first, already carrying their rifles over their shoulders. Along the pathway and the place where the snow had been shoveled away in the churchyard, moving around the cross, the snow was rough like an uneven floor made of glass. Divinangelo spat and his spit immediately turned to glass. They scoured the sky: a perfect, chilling calm. All the bare woods were stiffening under white clots of snow. The monastery's yellow walls were the color of a cadaver.

The boy went out in his tall boots and big fur hat, clumsy as a bear cub. Franzè's threat—go away or I will kick your ass—was so ferocious that the boy grimaced at him with his most insolent look and went headlong inside.

Every voice and motion echoed back into the openness as clear as the sounds in a tomb. Suddenly, very close by, the baby was heard wailing, as if she had been laid near a window. Across the churchyard, the steps of the two men grew louder. Frosted, broken branches exploded in the air like shots. From the beginning, all around, sounds were amplified. A sense of exposing oneself, of standing out before the whole world. The cross was stretching out its menacing arms.

Shortly after, Annaloro and Alleluia went out, holding their weapons and dragging their feet. They joined the other two, following instructions. Firing squad: all together, all responsible. Except old Baboro, who looked like he could not stand on his feet; he was silent, not responding, in a heap by the fireplace. The boy was his assignment and he was keeping him by his side, almost covered with his wide cloak.

When the condemned woman and the priest appeared, the firing squad was already lined up under Vanzi's command. Their heads turned simultaneously. Much to their surprise, she was well coiffed, she had pulled her hair back into a sleek bun, and she was wearing a peasant dress just like one of their women. She moved forward with dignity in her simple clothes, pale, taking brusque short steps that were stiff yet not uncertain. They were reassured immediately that she would not flee, screaming, and force them to chase her through the churchyard.

The men and the priest are not looking at each other. But he is talking. They have stopped. They seem not to notice the men lined up there. Utterly surprised but standing stiffly, the men see her bending down. Leaning on the priest with one hand, at a slant, broken, she takes off her shoes. Jesus, she thinks that they would take them off her feet, afterward. She is always the same, doesn't trust anybody: never ask a man too much if it's not absolutely necessary.

It was all terribly real, like a sculpture in relief against the dirty white surroundings, with clear outlines, embossed, and at the same time somehow unlikely. Breaking through the silence and immobility came a shriek from Annaloro, who had thrown away his rifle and run toward home. That's exactly what he said: "toward home." Inside the monastery, away from that situation, safe.

Two of them brought him back. Nobody was allowed to stay out of it.

4. The woman and the priest have started walking again. Like a broken, then mended, film that begins to unreel again. Her yellow wool socks in the snow and the priest's black feet. Next to the woman, now bigger, he looked small, scrawny, and crooked. He carries the crucifix. The brass shines in the minuscule sacred body that was touched on Christmas Eve by the fingers of the same men who are now getting ready to shoot. They kissed it, too. That thin, twisted, cold little corpse.

They slowly move forward on the shoveled path. Across the way, the cleared space waits for them. It will never end, they won't get there. At the command, the priest stops, holding out the crucifix in his hands. She continues. Alone.

Alone she goes and places herself before the rocky wall, turning her large, monumental back, her head lifted as if she were searching the sky. Turned backward. But she refuses to be blindfolded and turns around, waving her hand to invite them to hurry. As if she were giving them the go-ahead. Vanzi, dangling the black rag, returns to his position, limping on his lame leg. Lame from the war. His boots resound with harsh uneven thumps.

And at that moment, forcing an abrupt return to reality, a cry burst out: the kid, the kid. It was frightening and sounded as if it spread to the whole world. The kid was at the doorstep and as Vanzi brandished his gun, he went right back into his hole. Vanzi put the gun back in the holster, and then took it out again. He had shown his bald head, as yellow as a stone, then covered it again. He moved senselessly about. The woman, who had once again turned to face the wall, was standing stooped but still. Her head was no longer visible. She seemed to lean on the wall, as if she had taken ill.

I probably was the first to notice, or maybe I was the only one to notice right away. A desperate spectator, paralyzed but with all my senses alerted. The snow, dirtied. She could not make it. Fear loosens the bowels; the extreme offence. But, Christ, in that same moment, horrified, I was able to understand. That was blood. A hemorrhage.

Then everything happened with a fatal rashness. The men moved their hands mechanically. Their shaky, numb hands pressing against the metal of each weapon, so cold that it bit the skin. Vanzi was there, open-mouthed, he unleashed the commands from the black hole of his mouth. The firing was loud, rattling, repeated, and endless. The priest had thrown himself down on his knees, his face on the crucifix.

Franzè and Vanzi rushed over. Franzè arrived first, crouched down, bowing his tousled head, spiky, as if his hair were standing on end. The kid was coming in his tall, up-to-the-groin boots, rushing with his legs apart, with a silent, slanted step. Vanzi was still holding the gun but had stopped halfway. Nobody was prompt enough to halt the kid; we were all stunned. *Uhuu*, he was crying out next to

Franzè, with his arms open, showing his bony wrists in the frayed sleeves — two little paws stretching out. *Uhuu*, lifting his head under the prickly fur hat. He was the cub of our wolf pack, howling out the ravenous despair that was burrowing endlessly into our bowels.

The black pile on the ground was shaking. Franzè shouted, "C'mon c'mon!" to Vanzi, whose feet seemed nailed in place. He rushed to grasp the gun out of Vanzi's hands and came back at a crooked run. "Go away!" the boy screamed and hurled himself against him. "She is alive, leave her alone." Our wolf cub howled again. We were horrified. Franzè was trying to aim the gun at her for the coup de grâce while with the other arm he was pushing away the boy. Getting up from his knees, the priest rushed forward. And finally the men, too, moved again, throwing their rifles down. Darting out, the boy was trying to grab the gun with both hands. The gun fired. Then fired again, this time at the woman. The mountains all around slavishly echoed the shots.

The kid had fallen on the black skirt's hem, soaked and glued to the ground with her blood; he was twined against himself. The priest turned up the boy's head. The priest was holding that bare little head, very pale, that hung supine as a trickle of blood ran down from the corner of his thin, already relaxed lips, and the bony little arms in their frayed sleeves dangled inertly; the priest held him upright just as he exhaled his last breath.

As if the priest were exhibiting him. He was the lamb, we all recognized him at that moment.

5. In a great hurry, the men left the monastery. They went out in single file, burdened by their equipment, with their feet wrapped in bulky rags. First in line was the old man, prostrated, riding his mount. Alleluia the apprentice was holding the halter, tugging it over and over. The others followed. Last, Divinangelo was tottering behind in his ragged homemade shoes. Scattered footprints, heading every which way and dirty with trodden blood, could be seen here

and there on the snow. And the recently dug grave, only one, with one single cross made out of twigs and green branches that Annaloro had woven together. It looked like a wedding ornament. They did not look in that direction. Before they passed the corner, they turned, showing their grim or derelict faces with their dirty beards. They had not said farewell to the priest nor left any messages for their families. And the priest had gone back inside without turning back, handing them over to hell.

In the kitchen the lamp was still flickering, it would burn itself out completely. That yellowish clot I had kept pressed and inextinguishable under my eyelids all night. My eyes were hurting, I felt a migraine creeping in. I had always suffered from migraines, but never up there: the sort of immunity found in action. The fire was out. The night before nobody had taken care of covering the last embers with the pressed ash, as they usually did in preparation for reigniting a fire the next day by blowing the sparks. Now, after a hasty flare-up of humid twigs, only a little black ash remained.

On the ground, abandoned, the woman's shoes stood with their tips diverging as if in a walking position. The seminarian picked them up, tied the laces and threw them over his shoulder. I took the haversack with the bundle of papers inside, some candle ends and the jealously preserved matches. Without those, we could have taken the risk the others took and ended up dying. The poor thing had already woken up once and was quenched with the sugar mush. She whimpered again as she was picked up and wrapped in her mother's cloak. We set out. Once outside, he pulled the little milk canteen out of the snow where it was kept cool. The wailing faded as the baby fell asleep to the pace of the mountain walk.

We had set out without a word. I was following him. The frozen crust was thin, and at each step, as we sank into its cottony depths, it gave way with a creaking sound. A weary and systematic pace that got easier as we advanced. The snow started to melt as it shone under the sun.

I had no idea where we were headed, maybe nowhere. Were we running away too? He had mentioned the sheepfolds to the woman, but I doubted their existence and didn't think we would find people there. We found the cave. Under a pile of stones, exposed, more a shelter than a hideout. The Incoronata caves, which hid fugitives and partisans, were probably far higher in the mountains.

Our cave, which in the end turned out to be quite deep, enclosed a polished boulder with a hollow like a manger. He laid the restless bundle there, and she immediately unwrapped herself; uncovering a purplish little face poked from the edges, the most recent sugary rag still stuck to her chin. She had stopped wailing; she was screeching. A man gets stumped in such a situation. But not a priest, not that one. He left her screeching in the manger; it strengthens the lungs.

He was carefully looking around, then headed to a corner. There, still scanning around, he gathered some dry leaves and twigs that the wind had swept inside. Finally, searching his own invisible, deep pockets, he pulled out the bundle with the papers she had entrusted to him. He asked me for the matches. He had brought nothing with him but the baby, having faith in Providence. And, so it seemed, I was the first instrument of that. But he seemed not to see me; he acted as if I were not there, just as the others had. He hung the little canteen, the milk lapping inside, to a projecting rock and lit a fire under it. With those papers. He turned them into a fuel tablet; it slowly burned with a light blue flame. Heating the milk is a necessity.

Calmly he went and picked up the screaming baby and, sitting on the manger, laid her on his lap, throwing away the white rags wet with urine. The cloth had completely unraveled and underneath she was dressed in an outfit like a poor little doll's dress. I had always thought that under the swaddling she was as naked as the first time. Look, she even dressed her child. We are born into the world and then somehow we find something we can use to cover ourselves and food comes and life comes and we walk into it. A staggering simplicity. I was stunned.

The baby girl, in a little tumult, was tossing back and forth on his lap. He snapped his fingers above the little face all split and wrinkled from crying. An angry cry, at the top of her lungs. She wants food. She will get it. The priest was neither upset nor embarrassed; quite the opposite, confident and cheerful. He was laughing. A thought came to me — scandalous, innocent (yet natural nevertheless) — that he had under his cassock two cow udders and might feed her with those. At his signal, I handed him the little warmed canteen. My head was hot and I felt twinges of a sort of excitement.

I stayed there watching him twisting the sugary cloth into a wick, inserting it into the canteen's neck and, tilting the whole thing with close attention, letting it drip into the avid pink mouth. She stretches out to receive the milk, sucks and swallows, she already knows everything she has to do, knows it by herself. She grabs and sucks. Even brings her little tongue into line if too much milk drips. And she feeds on her mother's milk, she sucks as if it were her own mother's breast. At dawn, La Rossa, sitting on the little chair, while Annaloro held the bowl, had drawn her milk by squeezing a dark nipple with her big fingers. Milk squirts just like blood and has blood's consistency.

He wiped the baby's neck and chin with the corner of his handkerchief. He dripped the milk again. Less eager, her little mouth was gurgling now, filled and satisfied. And they stayed still, both sated, dozing off like beggars in the sun.

A glare mixed with a light blue smoke flooded the cave. Her papers, her testament, unfolding in dark ribbons, were sending off smoke. My conscience had no reaction. I only felt a burning sensation under my eyelids and inside my head.

6. When I spotted them they were already standing inside, staying close to the wall, squinting as they searched around. They were

three, two men and a boy. All of them wearing sheepskin gaiters and curly fur jackets like shepherds. The men with black beards, the boy beardless and redheaded. They looked neither armed nor threatening.

One of the men said, "We have been walking for two days."

And the other, "We arrived too late."

They addressed the priest as if they knew him already. And talked as if they were aware of what had happened.

They were coming from the Rapina. The Germans had dismantled the works for the cableway; only a collapsing barrack was left. And they could pass.

A man said, "We want to know the facts."

The priest briefly answered, "She died well."

And the other, "Did she leave a message?"

"A newborn is what she left. She died well."

They were interrupted by the screams coming from the manger. They turned and the oldest one crossed himself in that direction. They were carrying big flasks; there really was a sheepfold somewhere, and there were sheep and milk too. They had some. Cheese and wine too. They heated up the milk themselves using some left-over twigs and setting fire to what remained of the papers, now a black, dirty, wick. It was the oldest man who suggested diluting the heavy sheep's milk with a "little bit of fresh snow." They stared in amazement as the priest fed the baby.

They had crouched down on the ground, filling the cave and sending out a wild smell. It was hot. They questioned the priest again and never turned to me. I was flushed, I felt the blood rushing to my head and pulsing in my temples, but I registered every word clearly and sharply. They wanted to know if the monastery had been abandoned and which way "those" had passed. Whatever way they had gone — the men declared — they would not go far. They were going to block the fugitives at the Rapina, if that was their destination and they thought they would find the Germans there. We didn't know anything, but they knew everything. Only long afterward, I learned about the contacts between the partisans and Baba's farm.

"How many are you?" the priest asked.

"We're scattered in groups. We help two men at a time cross the front line through the mountain. There are women too. Here in this area it's not possible to stay any longer. The villages are kept under an iron fist. The violence is worse, dark things are happening. A village has been burned down and all of its people massacred. A German officer of rank opposed the slaughter and they executed him. They are afraid they are losing the war and it has turned them into beasts."

At the breath of their voices, puffs of burned paper fluttered and scattered through the air. As they reached the boy he would blow on them and follow them with his eyes. He caught one and it vanished in his hand. He was playing. He was probably thirteen or fourteen, a young beard was turning his cheeks gold. And his face was red, like the exposed part of his legs, from the heat of the fires in the mountain caves. His shoes were big, hard, and falling apart. I saw him staring at the woman's shoes that had been left on the ground, under the manger, in that same walking position. I nodded to him to take them. In one leap, he grabbed them. And immediately removed his gaiters and old shoes and put on the new ones, revealing a thin, pale foot.

I felt increasingly hot. The voices got confused in my empty head and were like meaningless noises. I stopped paying attention. And I thought I was falling asleep.

X

1. The transcript of the old papers ends here. Yellowed, musty papers, I can still smell them. An exhumation of ghosts. The last pages were written at the farm, during my convalescence; my hands still limp and my whole body shivering out of weakness. I wanted to finish my story, my testimony or whatever it was.

A mourning Baba, dressed in black, had looked after me. Her old, inscrutable face hovered over me without ever saying a word. I didn't learn of Baboro's death from her. Nor that I had been terribly delirious; three women couldn't hold me in my bed. Piercing pains had come back to me, all around me the bottleneck of the cave, sounds of wailing and screaming, the inextinguishable fire of a notebook, curling as it burned. Afterward, my memory opened up again. And it was burning.

I still have nightmares. At long intervals, but always with an intensity that frightens me. And always the same ones. The village completely in flames, an enormous torch, or people lined up — old people, women, children, a lot of children — and mowed down with a machine gun, and that repetition, endlessly echoed by the mountains, that deafens me in my sleep. (According to the last message Vanzi received, apparently it had been a real threat, or maybe just a feared one: at the monastery a partisan woman was being hidden.)

The life I lived is like a dream, dissolving when I wake up but leaving behind a sense of menace. The fear of the past. Going back to write about it may help exorcise it.

And the questions. Why I went up there. Why I joined those men. They were strangers to me and I was a stranger to them. I did not share their ideas, only the party membership card I was forced to sign. I went there unarmed and indifferent. Why? Maybe I should unearth the problems of my childhood and the solitude of my adulthood. Although at that time I was not alone, there was Zaira to love me. Docile and humble, a shy young peasant girl. But she was warm, she had that sensual instinct I've always lacked. And she comes to my mind, too, lovingly, with a voice that yearns for her gentleness, her timidity. I am grateful for my memories of her.

Or maybe I was drawn to adventure. A gray and flat life, spent always in the same village. People poor in spirit remain where they were born. I hadn't gone to war and I had come late to love — an existence at a slowed pace. The candle that burns slowly and gives off little light lasts longer. In fact, here I am, still alive. And I will die miserably in my bed.

But what's this, an old man's empty talk or a nightmare drawn out of my conscience? In any case, I have to go back, pick up the thread again, and carry out the exorcism until the end.

I was still at the farm when the last Germans, scattered by retreat, fled passing through the countryside. They were in tatters, their feet covered in sores. Not a woman refused water and food to the defeated enemy. Also let them wash their feet, and treated the sores, tearing off strips of linen as bandages. In the eyes of the women all the soldiers are equal, each came out of a woman's womb.

Even we, the reprobates, had been sheltered. A shepherd had carried me, feverish and unconscious, over his shoulders from the cave to the farm. One of the three men who came to the cave, I supposed. I never found out who saved me and if he survived. Two days later the others from the monastery arrived, carrying the dying old man on the mount. He died that very day in the arms of his old Baba. And everybody, desperate and exhausted, was sheltered there. We were staying on the first floor, downstairs the two Jewish families, and in the folds, the barns, the stables, were foreign soldiers and local Italian partisans, with their weapons at the ready. Later on we moved to the hideouts. But not for long. By twos and threes, we all went back, each to his own home, under the shield of the women. And there were no harsh reprisals around here. Only a mild ostracism that after a while faded away since we were all more or less related by blood, friendship, and mutual interest.

The women believed, or wanted to believe — and so did whoever was aware of those presences at the monastery — that the prisoner, the priest, and the boy had been deported by the Germans long beforehand. Those who knew the truth never said a word. And the monastery was hit by a reckless, as much as providential, bombardment. At the Rapina the cableway barracks had been set on fire; bones and the metal parts of uniforms were found (and a belt with a still-readable *Gott mit uns*) together with crusts of sheepskins and burned boot soles. Everything had been thrown into a mass grave under a single cross.

The aluminum canteen was never found and I never have believed that the young man and the baby girl died.

2. An episode that remains obscure to people spoiled the first liberation day. It has been told a thousand times and some people still recall it without understanding it.

We had spent the night awake, between rumblings and blasts, waiting for the final explosion that would have blown up the bridge. We were certain it had been mined by the Germans while they retreated, just as they mined the little power station that turned off our lights, a harmless sawmill, some scattered, solitary cottages in the country and their empty stalls. Once the bridge was blown up, the road downstream would be closed, isolating the village and the whole area upstream.

But at dawn, in a deep, incredible silence, through the misty fields, the high piers of the bridge appeared to rise intact out of the night's shifting vapors. And shortly afterward a scorched man, screaming like a lunatic, brought the news that the Germans had disappeared and the Allies were coming.

From the houses, the hideouts, the countryside, the mountains, a crowd overflowed into the village square at the call of the ringing bells. Last, with women and children came those strange foreigners who were so different from the locals, and so mournful, closely knit together into a timorous and cautious group. Somebody had brought them there from the farm, and then had eventually disappeared into the frenzied crowd. Everyone was out, shouting and cheering, throwing up their arms, running here and there to look for each other, to find each other again. The men who were hiding out, the local partisans and foreign soldiers, with their straggly beards, their scorched faces, wearing unmatched clothes and loaded with weapons, looked like the bandits from the old stories. Every incoming group would announce itself by shooting in the air. Only the next day the advance guard of the victors, motorized and well equipped with uniforms and arms, reached the village.

In the middle of the celebrations the episode occurred that remained incomprehensible to people and came to be marked with a shadow of resentment. Suddenly, among the shouts and the bell ringing, a rumor spread. Those dark fellows who looked mournful, that close-knit group of unknown people, strangers to all, after being pushed and tossed around in the crowd, had found a wide-open, empty warehouse, gone in and barricaded themselves. Squeezing together behind a counter, the children holding tight to their mothers—beautiful children and beautiful women with dark, curly hair—they seemed ready for a conflict. And two dark skinny men among them drew revolvers and aimed.

The locals had flocked together there, curious at first, then appalled, without understanding. For certainly those people, like many others, had been hidden and fed and protected by the village. The locals were indignant about such a reaction and became menacing in turn. It was a reciprocal misunderstanding, between rancorous and mistreated animals, one that could explode at any minute. The partisan leader, also a foreigner, the one they called "Davide," made a timely intervention. Ignoring the revolvers, he threw his weapons to the ground, went into the warehouse, and talked to those men. They immediately lowered their arms.

They thought they would find the Americans and had been scared by the uproar. But that did not explain anything, not to the locals and those in the surrounding countryside, not at that time at least. And not even when they learned of the monstrous genocide. But those men—people said—how could they be so afraid if they didn't yet know about it?

The next day the first victorious jeeps arrived. The Americans respectfully picked up the Jewish refugees in their command cars and drove them away. No news came about the priest and the child, neither in that period or any later one. A lot of people had disappeared. Bombings and deportations. Burned villages, decimated populations. And after that people wanted to forget. But one cannot forget.

I have searched for the child my whole life. I have pictured her at various ages, presuming I could recognize her by some sign, by an intuition. Wherever I went, I would look at the small children to see if there were little girls with plenty of hair, shaggy black hair, and the liveliness and strength I thought would be hers. In the city, my fascination with little girls, my desire to get close to them, to offer them a candy, has even been misinterpreted; the girls would be pulled away from me, with suspicious and scandalized, not to say menacing, looks.

And eventually there were dark-haired teenage girls in the street, teenagers in the queue of an orphanage, some servant girls at the market, and especially young lay sisters or, as years passed, nuns. I would go to the city wandering with that idée fixe: what happened to her? In the city I would go to the bus terminal or down to the rail-way station, searching the incoming passengers, in case there was a female stranger . . . . Once they set up a traveling fair and at the rifle range there was a very curly-haired and provocative gypsy girl who was handing out the rifle aggressively. I regret not being able to man-age a weapon. She herself skillfully could take up the rifle and shoot and hit the target. Later a thought came to mind: could she have turned into a terrorist?

At a certain point I calmed down. I was already old and said to myself: maybe she died back then. Her mother's milk probably turned sour, then the heavy sheep's milk, the cold, the strains of the journey: a bowel or chest pain and a baby dies in a moment. I wanted to convince myself of that. But to this day any woman with thick dark hair makes my heart leap.

3. I can hardly believe I am so old. When I can walk for hours with-out feeling tired. When I devour books and read again and again my favorite ones, like my small, ragged Dante that I always carry in my pocket. When I hold the pen and my mind races. Races backward in time, into memory. But all of a sudden, it gets stuck. Not on the facts: on a single word, usually the most common and obvious one. To retrieve it I need to wait until it comes back unexpectedly. I write words down anywhere I can and so I end up losing them again. I should keep a notebook, or some file cards; get organized. Untidi-ness does not suit old age.

And the insomnia. I can't find any comfort in my bed and my own bones make me ache. Or instead I sleep too much, a deep cataleptic sleep and I wake up stunned with a heavy, empty head. Since I was young I've always been slow to wake and in a bad mood when I do. But in old age the body's vital spirits lack the harmony they have in youth. Our animal structure, so perfectly planned around the seed of death. And that is where it is headed.

The physiological memory of certain sensations is now gone.

What was love, what was sex like? I try in vain to remember the sensation of feeling full of semen like an ear of wheat. When was the last time? Decline inadvertently squeezes out the last drops of life's honey.

I go out to take long walks. I am still thin and, in spite of my knock-knees, nimble. I wander through the countryside; I like the smell of the air, of the earth, of the animals. I smell the burned branches and the still warm dung. Nature's smells are primordial up here, in spite of the steady stream of cars in the village and the factory chimneys downstream. On every roof, even on the country houses, the crosses of the TV antennas. I prefer the radio.

I like the autumn. Things fading out in the gauziness of the season that draws to an end. Walking through grassy paths, under a pale, wet sun on the soft, dead leaves, with that smell of humus, to which our body will return. I want to be buried right in the ground, naked and wrapped in a sheet. Here you still can do that, here you don't end up poured into an urn that will end up in one of many wall niches.

Once I went back up to the monastery. Ten years later. Making two stops on my way up, one by the farmhouse. Baba was still there, decrepit and almost blind, but as authoritarian as always and surrounded by a band of grandchildren and great grandchildren. She recognized me with the touch of her fingers and wanted me to sleep in her wide marriage bed with its rustling pallet. We did not exchange a single word. When I left she granted me a big sign of the cross just as her late, much blessed and lamented husband used to do.

I reached the monastery alone and without a horse, but followed at a distance by two of Baba's sturdy grandsons. I gazed for a long time at the massive skeleton. The bombs had demolished the roof and damaged the internal structures. The main walls, stuck in the rock, had been lightly touched. And the overall plan was visible: cells, hallways, rooms, kitchen, and church. The maimed low altar wall was still standing. Only some dark brown traces like roots remained of the wrecked choir. Century-old wood had been burned in the fireplaces in the days when everything was burned to get some warmth and to cook some field greens. The old, crumbled stones had been collected as time went by to rebuild the houses and eventually to erect new walls. It was impossible to find the site of the grave in the ravaged, tormented ground with its sheaves of nettles and tangled bushes. So many times I had thought about the wolves, ravenous wolves digging at the grave. In the winter we spent up there we did not see any in the mountains. When man turns into a wolf, the wolves stay away from man.

4. I have always been a hypochondriac, therefore a loner. Or vice versa? Satisfied with the inexhaustible pleasure of reading. (And yet while I was up there, I never read a single line, I was busy living.) Even the only woman with whom I've ever had a long-term relationship never really came into my life. We never lived together. If she hadn't died young, I might have married her. She loved me. I remember her with sweetness and regret.

The only time I lived with others was at the monastery. Even now, in fact more than ever, just the idea of living a common life with strangers, of sleeping in a shared room with another person, overwhelmingly disgusts me. I did it back then. I still have to understand exactly why.

In the village, people probably now consider me to be a harmless eccentric. They are all very respectful; they seem to think I have been a good schoolteacher, even if I never used the stick — the parents themselves not only gave me permission to use it; they encouraged me to use it, for they were persuaded of its effectiveness. When my fellow villagers see me, they make a point of greeting me lavishly. Young and old men, whom I can't recognize, raise their hats smiling: old pupils of mine. As boys they would not run away to hide when they saw me coming, as their families would have expected. Maybe they too were affectionate toward me. Besides, I have always been dedicated to my job, which I liked, and maybe I was good at it, even gifted. They were glad to come to school, they would have come on Sundays too.

I've had no more contacts with the men at the monastery, not even exchanging greetings, on the street we avoided looking at each other. I have never seen them together. And one by one they have disappeared.

The first was Franzè. Like many others, after a while he had been rehired as a guardsman. His past record as a man of violence wasn't held against him; on the contrary, he came to wear a despondent look. And he was a real sleuth against the poachers and the wood thieves who were infesting the nearby woods. He was indeed re-admitted to society with full honors. But he could be seen around without his rifle and with his peaked cap pulled down over his face. A man who doesn't look anyone in the eye. The old Franzè, the one who carried his rifle straight over his shoulder, the peak of his hat boldly lifted up on his forehead and the short cloak fluttering, was gone. Not long after, he turned down the job.

His wife had restored the barbershop. The resourceful Menina replaced the mirror and the broken glass; she herself put on a coat of paint and polished the tools. Such a smart woman, she talked to anybody and told the story and explained it all. In good faith, or lying to cover her husband, she always claimed that at the monastery they were not in league with the Germans, quite the opposite . . . . But they could not have prevented those devils from deporting the boy along with a woman and a priest, both just passing through. And they had been within a whisker, she would claim, of all being shot at the last moment. Nobody ever showed up to prove her wrong.

The first returning customers tried to get more precise details and reports from Franzè. Wizened and bald, with just a few gray curls left on top, with his always-bristly cheeks and a haughty expression, he would respond in monosyllables. But the customers soon realized that if he got distracted his hand would shake and so nobody ever went back to get a shave. One day he was seen again with the rifle over his shoulder and his peaked cap pushed back, heading out of the village, into the woods. And his hand did not shake when, down on his knees, he shot himself in the mouth.

Alleluia fell into his own trap. The brute that fascinated our little pup up there. The appeal that violence wields over children. The kid was looking for shelter next to another weak body at night, but he followed the strongest one by day. He used to follow him into the stable to look after the animals, until I forbade that under the excuse that the mule could kick him. I had found them, as usual, roaring with laughter. Alleluia used to talk about animals, he had lived with them. That time he was telling about a dog of his. He got himself a dog. Not for companionship, he specified, but to keep guard when he was going around to castrate pigs (he had already explained to him how he did it) and some nights he had to sleep in the barns. A tax on dogs was enacted. He could not pay it. So he takes the animal—meek, it let him do whatever he wanted—and hangs it on a hook on the stable wall. An hour passes, two hours pass, time passes, and he forgot about it. When, suddenly, ruffled and all lopsided, the dog shows up again. The thin rope had broken. He is dazed. But the animal totters up to him and licks his hand. He had to find a stronger rope. "I," says the child, just to keep up, "kill flies and spiders. I have stoned two lizards and a toad." To kill: an act of power. But I was struck myself with the simplicity and naturalness of the fact.

Afterward, Alleluia had not stayed at the farm with Baba, subjected to the woman's domain. He took the mule and went back to his hovel made of piled up stones. He owned a cart and he carried loads on commission: sand, cement, bricks, hardware, even the monastery rubble. Reconstruction was under way. The loads were too heavy for the broken-winded, exhausted animal. On the slope of the village you could hear curses and heavy blows. Instead of a whip Alleluia used a sort of club and the blows resounded against the backbone. Everybody was disturbed, but nobody dared to set himself against that bully, he had listened only to old Baboro. People said he had cried over him, with real tears in his eyes.

He quit the old profession with the pigs. At first, because people no longer called for him, and when he was no longer able to geld the pigs, he was likely to disembowel them. He was living alone in that hovel with his mule and so he took out all his anger on the animal. (As I've taken out mine on the page?) The ill-treated animal could rest only when they went out to gather logs in the woods. They had been spotted, Alleluia hitting the trees, while the mule was grazing on the plants and eagerly nibbling.

The last time, two farmers, coming back through the maquis, heard a wail. The mule was quietly grazing, while the man was lying on the ground; his body was smashed. He had been kicked in the abdomen and his bowels were spilling out. People said that, as he fell, his golden earrings had been ripped off his earlobes and were still hanging from his bloody flesh. There was no more blood, but a shattered mess. The two men put together a litter with the already-cut branches, loaded him on that, and carried him by fits and starts down the mountain trail. He wailed all the way down, a sort of throaty howl — so they said — and yet he lived for several more agonizing hours. When I saw him he had fallen silent. Lying on the litter of green branches, deadly pale amongst the leaves, his head looked like the head of a pig, dressed with herbs and ready to be cooked. He radiated a placid animal innocence.

5. How we consider ourselves young at fifty, even sixty, when we are much older. But have I ever really been young? Now I am inexorably old. In that age when, looking back, you find the path of your memory studded with graves. A long cemetery with gravestones and half-erased epigraphs. All I can do is list the dead.

That makes two of us surviving. With a morbid interest, I have followed everybody's path toward the end. Short and hard, for just about everybody. Punitive? The young seminarian would have believed so, if not predicting it all. He let them go without turning back, condemning them to their hell. I stayed close behind his back and maybe I saved myself from that tacit sentence.

The peaceful Annaloro didn't want to be damned. Scared to death and dragged into the killing. He went back home too. And went back to cooking. He shut himself up in his house, better in the kitchen. His women would go out. Carrying a spade and a hoe, they went to work the land, the little they owned or that they worked as day laborers. All of them, five I think. And he would stay home and cook. He cooked and ate. When he appeared again, months later, sitting in an old, western-style rocking chair, out on his balcony, he was already enormous.

He had an inclination, almost a vocation, for cooking; during the war he had been a sutler. He learned how to do laundry with ashes but never had another chance to try delivering a child. His semen was faulty and his sisters and sisters-in-law remained spinsters. If I think about it, none of us has become a parent, afterward, as if we had all been marked by sterility.

In a couple of years he had put on chubby jaws and dewlaps around his neck, and carried a huge belly. All this while the laborers were getting lean, even the once-fleshy Madelona; they were all brawny and tanned and looked like young peasant men. And they took devoted care of him and provided him with food. He kept eating and getting fatter, until his fat choked him. He was only thirty-nine. Even after his death his swollen size was laughable. His women cried over him.

For some time I looked for them, or better, I looked for a way to see my comrades from the monastery, passing where I could probably meet one or the other of them, and I felt like an assassin continually drawn back to the scene of the crime. A sensation I've always felt, together with the burden of an uncertain yet conscious responsibility. I was and I remained a spectator, even gratified somehow.

Many times I crossed on purpose the out-of-the-way narrow street of the cobbler, but we never exchanged a single word, not even a sign of recognition. I was the one who looked at him; I was passing by that street to look at him. Little Divinangelo had reappeared out of the door with his small cobbler's bench, wearing the grumpy expression of an old spinster. Eventually he just sat still, and wrinkled, like a wooden puppet, or spent his time hammering in vain and making the nails leap on the bench. He roused himself only to threaten the curious kids coming closer to see his hen.

At first, a few forgetful old ladies had given him work — some last minute patching. But soon, out of necessity or out of compassion too, other clients had come back. Everybody has to make a living. But he did not show any humbleness; on the contrary, he always kept his bilious face turned to the side. And always frantically chasing off the children. The hen, too, perched on his shoulder, used to squawk and attack people like a rabid parrot. As much as he was wizened, with the proportions of a child, the hen was well-fed and full-breasted.

In the end, his neighbors would bring him supper, although he still spent time at the door hammering old shoes. Or maybe it was always the same old shoe. It seemed as if there were a mechanical puppet out there: he was hammering to a rhythm, the hen flapping her wings and taking off all around the box that served as his cobbler's bench. During the time he had left, he lived off charity without ever expecting any, and people remembered him thanks to the hen's arrogant clucking. One bowl for both of them. When he died, the animal made the announcement. It flapped out of the hovel, squawked and clamored until the women dared to enter. On a pallet, well built, clean, and dried out, lay a little mummy that looked a hundred years old. They fell to their knees and crossed themselves. And diligently cried over him, praying and complaining, as they usually do for anyone who has died.

Death is so highly respected because we will unerringly have our turn. Death belongs to us.

6. Vanzi too had resumed his job. He worked inside the post office so he wouldn't be noticed, behind his brother who stood in for him, and so he never appeared at the window. He was holed up in the back and all that could be heard was the sound of him using the stamp. When his brother died, years later, he had to come out in the open again. After all, he was the official. Head down, he attended the customers at the window, speaking only when it was required. The "tan tan" sound of the stamps now become one with him, was all there was to his voice.

A speechless man. Even at home — people said — he communicated by stamping, he called his wife and children by banging the table with sharp blows. People had forgotten his political past and over time he was known only as "the stamper." He made precise, sharply impressed stamps, without the slightest flaw or flabby outline. Perfectly readable, as if they were printed from a new linotype machine. He had turned into a machine. A machine to stamp papers with the state seal. Of the new Republic.

But after a while the crazy aspect of that behavior emerged. At first people smiled about it, as if it were a small, harmless mania. Here he goes, they would say as they heard from the street, in a silent pause, the tight sequence of those sharp blows. And the young late-night revelers would stop together to listen, snorting. He is still there, our postmaster is still shooting. He was firing blanks. The guy who said it first prompted the idea, a queer, absurd idea: that he was not stamping piles of mail — so much mail was not possible — but instead nothing. Not nothing at all, of course; maybe a random paper, a newspaper, scrap paper retrieved from the basket. The short pauses probably were due to a change of stamp. He had an assortment, in the wooden stamp holder, from which he meticulously pulled them one at a time, examining their condition and blowing off some imaginary fleck of dust before resuming the shooting. By day in moderation — and never before the public; at night, hopelessly, insanely, and shut in there. So the official's obsession was revealed.

Anyway, in the village nobody really paid attention or was surprised; people simply gave a wink, out of amusement and kindness. Eh, we each have a screw loose, we each can lose track of a Friday. And people get used to everything and by that time nobody really paid attention to that thumping noise. Until it stopped.

He had retired. And so the stamping was over. He can't possibly take home the stamps; state office stamps can't be tampered with. By then, his wife had died, his children had married and left the village; Vanzi was left by himself. What is he going to do? Well, he has started wandering around. Although he's not at all sociable, he goes from one house to the next. He doesn't speak. Walks in, dragging his leg, sits down, and counts the buttons. Yes, buttons. He counts all the buttons he happens to be wearing. On his jacket and vest, even on his shirt. He runs his hand over them, without looking, and moves his fingers up, and then back down; he counts and recounts, up and down, quickly moving that hand like a small machine. For hours, relentlessly.

We have Charlie Chaplin's tramp. He doesn't make us laugh.

I am the only survivor. I have passed half of my last decade, provided that I do reach my eighties. I look around and it all seems another world. But has it really changed? It was overturned: "The more things change, the more . . . " as the old folks say here with their crafty wisdom. In other words, it is always the same.

In fact I find myself at ease, although I now have survived several generations. Not that I actually participate, only as a misanthropic observer. And always extremely curious. It is a world I recognize. It is somehow even congenial to me.

Wars, we hear and talk only of wars. Apparently more than a hundred wars since then have broken out on the face of our bellicose planet. (Dante's "threshing-floor that makes us so ferocious.") In addition to those taking place right now. Attacks, claims, chains of reprisal that cause, fuel, and follow the conflicts. Everything repeats itself everywhere with the historical monotony of human relations. And now we fear a final conflagration.

So far nothing has changed, my testimony is still relevant. There is only one new phenomenon: drugs. Among the youngest. I learned it from the news. And I could find a connection.

But this is the last page of this story. A bundle of paper. A volume of paper. A book? Have I written a book?

Well, after all, I knew it. Maybe in the beginning I didn't know I knew it. When I thoughtlessly went to the monastery with those men. An adventure, but a passive one. An adventure, anyway. Now I know that I went there because I wanted to write a novel of the people. To come out of my private interests, the lamentations I wrote out in verses, never-lived loves, bookish experiences, in the narrow corner from which I had not changed my horizon. (A corner of the earth that nevertheless already contained everything.)

I wanted to tell about life, passions and anxieties, war and blood. I carried inside me the will of a writer, one who observes everything and stores everything and broods over it all. Not the lukewarm tone of the Gospels. Mine was the witness's detachment. As a spectator.

The writer is a fearless spectator. A psychological voyeur. And that was my way of getting involved in life.

When, at night in my cell by candlelight, I was taking note of the events of the day, and grasping people in their acts and words, I did not feel the cold, I forgot the other presence in the cell; I entered into a state of excitement, a wave of mysterious pleasure. I felt that way again while I was transcribing it all.

Have I actually made a transcription? And at that time did I always stick to the plain and humble style of the chronicle? A document, of course. But I was often overwhelmed with that excitement, that pleasure of fixing it on the page. And it happened again with these new pages. Without altering the facts, I have tried to see into them, to investigate the people. To turn them into characters. They did not always express their thoughts in words. I was not always physically present. Maybe the woman did not pour out that flood of words at once. But she could have said them all, she held them inside her.

I am seized with confusion and doubts. If I try to read it again, I almost can't distinguish between the truth and fiction. Reality is overshadowed and ghosts take shape. Maybe art lies in this osmosis. And this is the pleasure of creating. Maybe I am a writer.

And now? Should I abandon, destroy everything? Now it starts to hurt me. Because I am getting attached to this — it was painful — a part of me and others, a slice of humanity, a bleeding shred of life so filled with death. Life and death fertilize each other.

I will pass away, but may the papers outlast me. I want to save them. I will make a well-tied and sealed bundle and leave precise instructions. To be sent to . . . To be handed to . . . To be published. After death, one is accepted. And maybe considered.

One of the poor women who take care of my house will have to call a priest, even if he's not been asked for. I will hand him the bundle with my last will. May it become a book. The story remains open, though; a book is never finished.

But what happened to the child?